"Jess, why are you here?"

She'd come into his room in the middle of the night and he'd grabbed her and pinned her against the wall. He let her go when he realized who it was.

"I came to protect you. You're still weak. And it's not safe for you to be alone." As she spoke, she stepped toward him till she was mere inches away.

"You can't keep saving me, Jess. And you shouldn't be so close."

Dammit, he wasn't a robot, or a dead man—yet. When a beautiful woman wanted a kiss, he was ready to comply. But somehow not with her.

"Jess, I only have now, this moment. I can't promise—"

"I didn't ask for promises, Steve."

Throwing better judgment to the wind, he bent his head and kissed her.

That was when gunshots tore them apart.

JUDY CHRISTENBERRY

RANDALL ON THE RUN

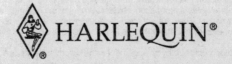

HARLEQUIN®

TORONTO • NEW YORK • LONDON
AMSTERDAM • PARIS • SYDNEY • HAMBURG
STOCKHOLM • ATHENS • TOKYO • MILAN • MADRID
PRAGUE • WARSAW • BUDAPEST • AUCKLAND

ISBN 0-373-22887-2

RANDALL ON THE RUN

www.eHarlequin.com

"Come on, baby," she called.

There was a loud *woof* before the arrival of her "baby," a golden–labrador retriever mix. He'd kept her company so she wouldn't forget home. Every morning she'd run with Murphy at her side, his tongue hanging out as he raced gleefully along.

With one last look, she locked the back door and reached for the garage door opener just as shots rang out. Jessica swallowed as a shiver raced over her. After all the warnings of her family, she hadn't had contact with any bad elements in Los Angeles since her arrival. Immoral elements, yes, but no gun-toting bad ones.

On her last night she ran into a gunfight? What were the odds?

She paused, but when she heard nothing else, she joined Murphy in her SUV and locked the doors before she pressed the garage door opener. Then she cautiously backed out. Everything seemed deserted, exactly as it always was.

Good. She just wanted to get away.

Flicking on her high beams, she started down the alley. Then she gasped when her eyes lit on a dark mass on the roadway. It looked like a body! She slammed on the brakes and took a second look.

It was a man. And he wasn't moving. Was he dead?

As much as her better judgment was telling her to

Chapter One

Jessica Randall was going home.

She breathed a sigh of relief when she'd finally loaded into her car all her personal items from the furnished apartment where she'd lived for three years.

Three years. She'd been awfully naive when she'd first arrived in Hollywood. Since then, she'd learned a lot about the movie industry—and it wasn't all good. In fact, the underbelly of Hollywood had soured her on living here. Dreams about home had gotten stronger and stronger until she could no longer relegate them to her subconscious.

It was night, but she figured she could get in at least five hours of driving before she'd have to stop and sleep. After all, in Hollywood, no one went to bed early.

Besides, she didn't want to stay here one more night.

CAST OF CHARACTERS

Jessica Randall—Three years in Hollywood couldn't rub off the Randall code. Jessica couldn't pass by a person in need without offering a helping hand—no matter what it cost her.

Stephen Carter—Someone wanted him dead—and had almost done the deed. But just when he thought he was a goner, a Hollywood beauty had come to his rescue.

Mike Davis—He was the sheriff of Rawhide and married to a Randall woman. He was also required by law to report a bullet wound. Could Steve trust this small-town lawman with the truth?

Marcus and Baldwin—They had been Steve's partners, but now they were out for Steve's blood.

Miguel Antonio—He was Steve's boss and the second-in-command at the Drug Enforcement Agency. Before he could make his move, Steve had to decide. Was this D.C. big shot friend or foe?

ABOUT THE AUTHOR

Judy Christenberry has been writing romances for over fifteen years because she loves happy endings as much as her readers do. She's a bestselling author for Harlequin American Romance, but she has a long love of traditional romances and is delighted to tell a story that brings those elements to the reader. A former high school French teacher, Judy devotes her time to writing. She hopes readers have as much fun reading her stories as she does writing them. She spends her spare time reading, watching her favorite sports teams and keeping track of her two adult daughters.

Books by Judy Christenberry

HARLEQUIN INTRIGUE
731—RANDALL RENEGADE
887—RANDALL ON THE RUN

keep driving, to leave Hollywood and all its baggage behind, she knew she couldn't. She had to stop. Leaving her engine running, she looked carefully around her before she slipped from behind the wheel.

In the bright beam of her headlights, she saw the man was still breathing, but bleeding heavily from his upper right torso. "Hold on, I'll call for an ambulance," she told him, though she didn't really think he heard her.

She turned then, but a strong hand grabbed her arm, holding her in place. A scream died in her throat as she looked down at the injured man.

"No! No ambulance."

"But you need medical help. I can't—"

His hand on her arm squeezed harder. "No doctor, either," he managed to say.

"What do you expect me to do? I can call the police but they'll—"

"No!"

A suspicious feeling settled around Jessica. The man was seriously injured, but he refused help. Why? Fearing the worst, she began to back away.

"I'm DEA undercover." Through his pain he managed to get the words out, but she could see the effort was a struggle for him.

"Then why can't I call the police?" She remained skeptical.

"I—I think my own people shot me. The police

will contact them…and I'll die. I won't be able to—to defend myself." The lengthy speech drained him, and he sighed deeply.

Jessica had no way to know whether his story was true or just another of Hollywood's fictions. But there was something about the man, something she heard in his voice, that made her take a chance. If what he said was true, she had to get out of this dark alleyway, and fast. "Do you want me to take you anywhere? Someplace safe?"

He nodded.

"You'll have to tell me where to go."

"Okay," he muttered, but his eyes slowly closed.

Jessica knew she had to do something about the bleeding, otherwise he wouldn't make it much longer.

She hurried to the truck and the first-aid kit her father had insisted she bring with her. "You might need it in Los Angeles." Just thinking about her father and his strength and courage steadied her nerves. She took the box to where the man lay and ripped his shirt open to expose a gunshot wound in his shoulder.

She was surprised to find a manila envelope stuck in the top of his pants.

"What's this?" she asked, almost to herself.

Again to her surprise, his hand grabbed the envelope, but he didn't have the strength to pull it from hers. "Evidence. It's…important."

"I'll take care of it. I won't let anyone see it." Her voice was urgent. She was afraid whoever shot him would come back to be sure the job was done.

He seemed to accept her assurance as his grasp loosened. She lay the envelope beside her as she began to tend to the gunshot wound, hoping the thick pad she held on the wound would slow the bleeding.

He cursed in a hoarse voice.

But she knew pressure was needed to stop the bleeding. Then she struggled to get him to his feet. When he was finally upright, though draped all over her, she led him to the SUV. He was a big man, and without his help she never could've gotten him up.

"Got to hide," he whispered in her ear.

Again shivers attacked her. She didn't know if it was from the words or the breath of hot air against her skin. "Okay. But first we have to get you inside. You're going to have to help me."

She'd gotten a couple of friends to help her put her mattress in the back of the SUV, with the rear seats folded down. Murphy used it as a comfortable bed.

Shoving back some of the clothes, she wedged the man in behind the front seat and lay his head on a pillow. All in all, she thought he'd be pretty comfortable. To be on the safe side she covered him with some of her clothes, and on his head, pulled down low over his face, she put a cowboy hat that she'd taken with her from Wyoming as a remembrance of home.

Maybe it was a little overdone, but she wasn't taking any chances.

Remembering her promise to take care of his evidence, she hurried back to the spot and grabbed the manila envelope. She slipped it beneath her seat in the SUV, out of sight.

When she got behind the wheel, she thought she caught some movement in the dark behind her. But when she looked around, she saw nothing; she told herself it was her imagination, and pressed down on the gas.

"Damn!" She'd forgotten to ask her passenger where he wanted to be taken. She leaned over the seat back, but even when she shook his leg under the clothes, he didn't answer.

So now what was she supposed to do?

She got on a freeway, or a parking lot, as they called them in L.A., headed in the direction she planned on going. At least he was safe in her car. When he woke up, she'd figure out how to get him where he needed to be.

About twenty minutes later, she wasn't quite as sure about his safety as flashing lights suddenly appeared in her rearview mirror. At the siren she carefully pulled to the side of the road and put on her hazard lights. She certainly hadn't been speeding. Why was she being pulled over?

After a quick check to be sure her passenger remained hidden, she rolled down her window.

A Los Angeles policeman approached her and she greeted him with her most charming smile. "Good evening, Officer. Was I going too fast? I didn't think so, but—"

"No, ma'am. But we've been looking for a perp in a robbery and the car kind of fit the description of yours."

For some reason, Murphy growled at the officer. Jessica realized the dog hadn't made any protest about her injured passenger.

"Well, there's just me and Murphy," she said, gesturing to her dog. "Unless the bad guy was a woman with a big dog, I think you've got the wrong vehicle." She noticed his eyes kept focusing on the piles of items in the back.

"You've got a lot of things in your vehicle. Big shopping trip?"

"No, not at all. I'm moving."

"No furniture?"

"No, I was renting a furnished apartment."

"I see." He still stood there, searching with his eyes. Finally, he said, "Mind if I search your car?"

She gave him an appalled look. "Yes, I do. It may not look organized to you, but I very carefully loaded my things so that nothing would get broken. I don't want you stirring things up. Anyway, it's not as if I could hide a—what did you call him, a perp?—in there."

"Okay, I guess not. Where are you headed?"

Jessica did some quick thinking. She hadn't turned off yet to head north, and she didn't think she wanted this man to know where she was going. "Dallas. I thought the best route would be to hit Highway 10 and go straight across."

"Yeah, that'd be best." One more look, then the officer tipped his hat, thanked her for being so patient and strode back to his vehicle.

She closed her eyes for a moment of thanksgiving after he eased his patrol car back onto the freeway.

Could her passenger have been telling the truth? She was beginning to think so. She drove cautiously for several exits, then pulled off to stop at a drive-in grocery. She went inside and bought some bottled water and a couple of snacks, the latter of which she shared with Murphy. Then she returned to the car and found her tool kit, another item her father had insisted on, and something else she'd saved. Her Wyoming license plates.

Quickly, she replaced the California license plates on her vehicle. Her shaking fingers slowed her, but it didn't take long. Then she got in and drove away from Highway 10. If her passenger had been telling the truth, she might be stopped again if she kept the same plates. Or if she stayed on the highway she'd told the officer she would be on.

Now she was headed for Nevada, Utah and then Wyoming, her home. Whenever the guy woke up and wanted out, she'd set him free. But she was heading home.

The last thing she did before she got back on the road was to give him some aspirin to control the fever she felt sure would follow.

About 3:00 A.M., Jessica pulled into a rest area, cracked her windows enough to let in air but not enough to let anyone have access to her car while she slept. She reached for another pillow for herself, and gave a blanket to Murphy. After checking on her still-sleeping passenger, she curled up and fell asleep.

When Murphy wanted out the next morning, he woofed gently, and she opened one eye. "Murphy, are you sure? I'd like to sleep longer."

He woofed again.

"Okay, okay." She sat up and rubbed her eyes. Then she remembered her passenger. She scooted over so she could reach his face. He was still asleep, but the fever was raging. She left him alone while she opened her door and got out with Murphy.

After her dog had relieved himself, she brought him back to the vehicle and got out more aspirin and a bottle of water. "Wake up," she whispered to the man, who didn't appear interested in waking at all. She finally got him awake enough to take more aspirin and a small sip of water. Then she left him alone again.

"Murphy, I'm going to the restroom. Keep guard of our friend, okay?"

She patted him on the head and slipped out of the vehicle, locking the door behind her.

When she came outside again, she eyed the pay phone. If she was going to call her cousin Caroline, now would be a good time, and no one would pick up her conversation, as they could on a cell phone.

She dialed the number for a collect call. When someone answered, she was afraid they wouldn't accept the charges, but she used her full name and the Randall part of it did the trick.

"Oh! Oh, yes, just a minute."

The operator said, "Hello, ma'am, will you accept the charges?"

When there was no answer, the operator said to Jessica, "Ma'am, I'm sorry, they won't—"

She was interrupted by a voice Jessica recognized. "Hello? Yes, we'll accept the charges."

"Go ahead, please," the operator said and clicked off.

"Caroline?"

"Yes, Jess. Where are you?"

"Some place in Utah."

"You're coming home?" Caroline's voice rose in excitement.

"Yes, but that's not why I called. Listen, Caroline, I have a—a person who's been shot."

"What? Jessica, what are you up to?"

"I'll explain later. I bound the wound tightly to stop the bleeding, and I've given him aspirin. I don't know if the bullet is out or not. Is there anything else I need to do?"

Since Caroline was one of two practicing doctors in Rawhide, Wyoming, her family's hometown, she knew Caroline could advise her.

"No, nothing else, except to take him to a doctor."

"He refuses."

"Why?"

"It's a long story. And I don't know how long I'll have him around. If he comes to, I'll probably drop him somewhere."

"This doesn't sound smart, Jess. He could hurt you."

"Not as long as he's passed out. But don't worry. I'll be careful. If I have to bring him home, will Mike have to report him being shot?"

"That's the law," Caroline said, her voice sounding ominous. "I'm going to call Uncle Brett right now if you don't explain yourself."

She immediately begged her cousin not to worry

her father, Brett Randall. "I'm being careful, I promise, Caro, but I have to get back on the road and there are reasons I can't talk about him on the cell phone. Someone might pick up the call."

"This is sounding worse, Jess, not better!"

"I know, but I promise I'll explain when I get there. Just trust me for a couple of days."

"All right, but no longer. And call back."

"I will. I'm going to call Mom and Dad to let them know I'm coming." Jessica breathed a sigh after she hung up. She'd been afraid of Caroline's answer. She knew the man needed a doctor, but she wouldn't take him to one against his will.

Unless he worsened, of course.

She hurried to her SUV as if her thinking such thoughts would make them come true. She opened the door on Murphy's side and pushed her dog to the driver's seat so she could lift the hat and clearly see the man's face.

He was handsome, in a rough way. He needed a haircut and a shave, but nothing could hide his sculpted features. No wonder he was in Hollywood, home of the beautiful people.

Luckily it appeared the bleeding had stopped. She got out the first-aid kit again. If she rebandaged him, she could use the antibiotic cream, which might stave off an infection.

The ugly sight of his wound reminded Jessica

why she hadn't gone into medicine, like Caroline had. And her checkbook always taunted her for not going into accounting, like her sister, Tori, had.

In fact, in addition to her flair for the dramatic, it was because she had no other skills that she'd turned to acting. But at least she'd proved herself. She'd stayed in Hollywood until she got a role in a major film. That way her family wouldn't think she was a failure when she came home.

Just as she was finishing binding the wound again, the man moaned.

"It's all right," she whispered soothingly. "You're safe."

She was sure he heard her because the tension in his body went away. She covered him up to his neck and lay the hat on his stomach so she could reach it quickly if she got pulled over again.

They were only a few miles from Cedar City, Utah, a town in the southern part of the state. When she reached the outskirts, the hat went back over the man's face so she could pull through a fast-food restaurant drive-through and get breakfast for her and Murphy. She didn't think her passenger would be up for any food just yet.

Once she'd done that, and Murphy was busy munching his sausage and biscuit, Jessica began talking to her dog, as she always did. He was her best listener.

"You know, Murph, I can't keep referring to him as 'the man.' Maybe we should give him a name. What do you think of Angus? He's got dark hair. He could be an Angus. Or maybe he's a cowboy, like the men in my family. Shall we call him Clint, in honor of Clint Eastwood?"

Murphy woofed his disapproval.

Jessica suggested several other names until a deep voice said, "Steve."

She almost drove off the road as she stared at her dog. Then she realized the sound had come from behind the seat. She did pull to the side of the road then. "You're awake."

"Yeah," he said, just barely above a whisper.

"I should give you some more aspirin. Are you in pain?"

"Yeah."

Well, he was a big conversationalist, wasn't he?

She put the aspirins in his mouth and then lifted his head slightly so he could drink the water.

After a long drink, he sank back. "Where are we?"

She was afraid her answer would shock him. "Utah."

"Why?" he asked, his brow wrinkling.

"I was on my way home. You didn't tell me where you wanted to go, and I couldn't just let you lie there and bleed to death, so I brought you along with me."

"Too dangerous," he muttered.

"I think we're safe enough now. Though I did worry when the policeman pulled me over."

"When?"

"Last night in L.A. on the freeway."

"Why?"

Another one-word response. "He said my vehicle fit the description of one belonging to a perp who'd robbed a store. He wanted to search my car, but I told him no."

"How did you know you could refuse? Most people—"

"I asked a policeman who was a consultant on a cop show I did once. He told me."

"And the officer said okay?"

"Yes. He looked into the back and let me go. Then I gave him a phony destination."

"Plates. They can track—"

"Doesn't matter. I changed plates."

"How?"

"I kept my Wyoming plates for sentimental reasons. So, after he stopped me, I changed back to my Wyoming plates. And they haven't expired. Then I cut across to the highway that leads to Salt Lake City."

"You said Wyoming."

"Yes, that's where I'm headed. Do you want me to drop you off somewhere?" She was surprised at the reluctance she felt at turning him out on his own. She'd saved his life, after all.

"No, they won't look for me there."

"Who, Steve?"

He swallowed hard. "My partners. They shot me... I think my boss is in on it too. That's why I have to get to Washington."

"You're in no shape for that," Jessica told him. "Right now we're just trying to get you to a doctor in Wyoming—"

"No doctors!"

"If you'd let me finish, the doctor is my cousin."

"But they have to report it to—"

"The law, who is her husband. I'll explain everything, and he'll do the right thing." She hoped he didn't ask what the right thing would be. Mike would try to help, but that didn't mean he wouldn't report the wound.

"Okay."

It was as if she could read his mind. She was sure he was thinking he'd have time to get lost again, because it would take his enemies time to get to Wyoming. She didn't bother arguing with him.

"So, we'll be on our way, Steve. That is your name, isn't it?"

"Yeah."

"Are you hungry? I can stop—"

"No. Just drive."

So the man had a bit of an attitude. Jessica wanted to remind him that men usually went out of their way for her, not the other way around. Some men even found her attractive. Then she caught herself up. That was a Hollywood thought. She needed to remember how life was in Rawhide. She'd be home soon.

She got behind the wheel, gave Murphy a pat and started the engine, automatically locking the doors. Then she eased back onto a highway that didn't have a lot of traffic. It was a relief after Los Angeles.

They picked up traffic again as they got close to Salt Lake City. Steve had gone back to sleep, so she had no conversation to relieve the boredom of the drive, but she felt a growing excitement about going home.

For lunch she chose a restaurant this time, rather than fast food, because she thought she should get something for Steve. She locked him and Murphy in the car and went inside. After she placed an order to go, she went to the ladies' room. Then she returned to wait for their food.

It only took fifteen minutes, but she was impatient. Finally, she carried a big sack of food out to her SUV and put it behind her seat.

When she got in, she stopped Murphy from pawing through the sack. "No, Murphy, you have to wait. When we get to a park, I'll let you get out and eat your dinner."

On the other side of the city, she found a park that didn't have many people out in the middle of the day. She took out Murphy's steak and put it on the grass and led him to it. He began chowing down at once.

Jessica returned to the SUV so she could feed Steve the beef broth she'd bought for him. "Steve, can I prop you up so you can eat some lunch?"

"Yeah," he whispered, though she wasn't sure he was really awake yet.

She took the second pillow and got it behind him, then she opened the container and began feeding him the soup.

He kept sniffing, reminding her of Murphy.

"Why do you keep sniffing?"

"Because I can smell steak. I want to know how much of this slop I have to eat to get to the good stuff."

Chapter Two

After staring at him, Jessica said, "Sorry. The steak is for Murphy, not you."

"The dog? I need steak to help replace the blood I lost."

"No, you're still running quite a bit of fever. This is all you get for a while…unless you want to see a doctor?"

"No!" he protested, though his voice was weak.

She'd left Murphy's door open, and he jumped into the seat and put his head over the back of it.

"Damn it! He's big enough to be a horse!" Steve exclaimed.

"No, he's not. Murph, you're drooling on our patient. Sit!"

As always, Murphy obeyed her at once and disappeared from Steve's view.

"Now finish your broth so we can get on the road again," she said, trying to be patient.

"I don't want anymore," he grumbled.

"Don't be a baby just because you didn't get steak."

"That's not it. I—I need to use the facilities."

"Oh." After a minute she said, "I need to stop for gas. You can take care of things then. But first we'll need to take off that bloody shirt." She rummaged in the back of the vehicle and found an oversized zippered sweatshirt that had been her favorite on a damp morning.

With assistance from her patient, she carefully took off his bloody shirt, which she tossed in a trash can, and zippered him into the sweatshirt.

Steve was stoic through it all.

Next she put away his broth, ignored her own lunch and got back on the road. At what she thought was the last gas station outside town, she pulled in. After she stopped, she shook Steve.

"I'm awake."

"I'm going to put in the gas. Do you need help getting out?"

"No, but the dog's in the way."

"I'll move him." When she got out, she motioned for Murphy to come to her seat. She'd left her window down, and Murphy hung his head out while she pumped the gas and Steve slowly ambled over to the restroom. She thought everything was going well until the station attendant stuck his head around the back of her SUV.

"Howdy," the man said, grinning too broadly.

"Hello." Her hand loosened on the gas handle and she almost spewed gasoline everywhere. She looked over her shoulder to see if she could see Steve returning.

"You headed to Wyoming?"

She stiffened. Even without Steve, she didn't like to tell strange men where she was going.

"I saw your plates and guessed," the man added, still grinning.

"Yes, I'm going back to Cheyenne, my hometown." She patted herself on the back for coming up with another good story. But then that had always been one of her few talents.

"I been there once. It's a nice city. Lots smaller than Salt Lake." He moved closer.

"That's true. Are you from Salt Lake City?"

"Naw. I move around. Don't like to stay in one place all the time." He kept staring at her.

Through the windows, she saw Steve coming back. She smiled at the man, wanting to keep his attention on this side of her vehicle so Steve might be able to get in unobserved. "I like Salt Lake City, but I have to leave because my mother is sick. She wants me to come take care of her."

"Aw, that's too bad. But you'll be coming through a lot to visit your friends, I bet. Will you stop by here again?"

"Probably. This is a good location." She replaced the nozzle in its holder and opened her purse, taking out some bills. "May I pay you?"

"You sure can. I'll go get your change."

"Oh, just keep it. You've been very kind."

She opened her door and jumped in, moving Murphy over to make room. Unfortunately, Steve hadn't gotten in the back. He was sitting in the front passenger seat. She shoved Murphy in the back so they could get out of there.

"Do you think it's wise to sit up in the front? I can't hide you if you're up here."

"We're almost in Wyoming, aren't we?

"In an hour or two. But I'm afraid that man was suspicious. He asked where we were going."

"He was just hitting on you," Steve said.

"I hope that's the reason, because you look like you've gone through World War III."

"I don't think he even noticed me, right, Murphy?"

Murphy had hung his head over the seat, almost resting on Steve's left shoulder.

"I can't believe he didn't bark when I first put you in the car. He growled at the policeman," Jessica said, frowning.

"He probably realized I was injured and couldn't hurt you."

Jessica didn't answer because her attention was focused on the rearview mirror.

"What is it?" he asked quietly.

"There's a car coming up on us fast. I'm worried—" She broke off as the car roared past them. They could see two teenagers in the car laughing hysterically.

She breathed a big sigh of relief. When she turned to look at Steve, he scarcely seemed aware of her panic. Pain was visible on his face.

"I'm having trouble sitting up," he managed to say.

She eased the car off the road. "There's a button that will lower the seat for you." She released her seat belt and leaned over him to find it, which put her very close to him, a fact she noticed at once. Fortunately, she got the chair lowered quickly. Then she reached in the back seat for the pillow and put it under his head. Feeling his forehead told her his fever was still high. She pulled one of the blankets over him.

"Better?" she asked.

"Yeah." His eyes were already closed and she didn't think he'd be awake for long.

Jessica pulled back onto the road and pressed down on the accelerator. She wanted to be in Wyoming as soon as possible.

WHEN SHE NEXT STOPPED for food, they were in Wyoming. She'd headed north, working her way across the state. The sun had set and she'd considered stopping somewhere to sleep, but she'd decided to keep driving until she reached Rawhide.

Beside her, Steve hadn't uttered a sound since she'd gotten him settled hours ago.

She pulled the cover up over his shoulder, entered a burger place drive-through and placed an order.

The girl at the window looked at Steve. "What's wrong with him?"

"He's not feeling well. He has a cold."

"It's probably the cold front coming through. My mom always gets a headache when we have a change of weather."

"Are they expecting snow?"

"In the mountains and farther north they are. Not here, though."

"I see. Thanks," Jessica said as she took the drinks and bag of food, then pulled away quickly, wanting to be out of sight of the inquisitive young woman.

"People ask a lot of questions, don't they?" Steve muttered.

"So you're awake?"

"Yeah. And hungry."

"As soon as we get out of town, I'll stop and get you your food."

"Do you think you could raise the seat a little?"

Jessica thought about that. Reaching over him would practically put them body to body again. Not a good idea. "How about I put another pillow under your head? After you eat, you're going to want to lie down again. That'll be easier."

"Okay."

When they were out of town, she pulled off the road and dug out Murphy's food first. Opening up the paper the burgers were wrapped in, she put them both out for Murphy.

"The dog gets served first?"

"If I don't fix his first, he eats mine...or yours. Do you want that?"

"Nope."

"Now, here's your hamburger and fries. I'll put your drink in the holder. If you can't reach it, let me know."

"We're not going to stop to eat?"

Jessica shook her head. "Didn't you hear the girl? There's a front coming in."

"But she said it wouldn't snow here."

"We're not staying here. We're heading north."

JESSICA HAD BEEN driving for several hours. By her calculations, she had only three hours to go. That was when she saw the first snowflakes in the glare of her headlights. Since she was traveling northeast, she had hopes of outrunning the brunt of the storm.

Some winters the snow held off until mid-November, but here it was only a few days into the month and it was snowing hard already. The farther north she drove, the heavier the snow fell. She pushed a little harder on the accelerator.

The sight of flashing red lights in her rearview mirror made her stomach roil. Immediately she slowed and pulled off the road. Then she made sure the blanket was pulled up over Steve's shoulder.

It was too late to hide him.

She lowered her window partway and waited for the policeman to reach her side. "Good evening, Officer," she said.

"Evening, ma'am. May I see your license and registration?"

"Yes, of course." She bent over and found her purse on the floorboard. Then she took out her license. Thankfully, she'd kept her Wyoming license in her billfold underneath her California license. Now she handed the man both.

"You have two licenses?" the patrolman asked in surprise as he examined the articles with the flashlight.

"I kept my Wyoming license when I got my new one in Los Angeles. Now I'm moving back to Wyoming."

"I see, Miss…Randall? Are you part of the Randall family in Rawhide?"

"Yes, I am. My father is Brett Randall."

"Well, Miss Randall, I'm proud to meet Brett's

daughter. You *were* driving a little fast, but I'm sure— Is there something wrong with your friend?"

Jessica swallowed. "Yes, my fiancé is suffering from the flu. That's why I was hurrying. I wanted to get home to Rawhide and not have to stop because of the snow."

"And you're bringing him home to meet the family? Well, I can see how that would be important. But you must promise me you won't go too fast and if you have to stop because of the snow, do so. I wouldn't want you to be wrecked in some ditch somewhere. Your daddy would never forgive me."

"I promise. I'll be careful."

"And be sure to reapply for another license, okay?"

"Yes, sir." Jessica sent him a thankful smile and watched as he walked back to his vehicle. Then she eased back onto the road again.

"Your family must be awfully important," Steve muttered.

"How long have you been awake?" Jessica demanded, grateful he hadn't spoken while the officer was there.

"Long enough to know you're my fiancée now."

Jessica gasped. "I—I just told him that because I didn't want him asking for your identification. Do you even have any?"

"Yeah, I've got— Hey, it's snowing!"

"That was why I was going too fast. Now I've got to be careful. He'll probably call Daddy."

"At least he hadn't gotten a bulletin about pulling you over from L.A. I was worried about that," Steve said with a sigh.

She leaned toward him and felt his forehead. "Your fever is rising again. If I give you a bottle of water and some aspirin, can you take them by yourself?" she asked.

"Of course I can."

She handed him the water, then dug in her purse with one hand for the aspirin bottle, which she gave him. "It's a child protection cap. Can you open it?"

"I'm not a child." The fever was doing nothing to assuage his attitude, obviously.

Steve worked on the bottle but had no success. Still, he never asked for help. After a while, she pulled the SUV over to the side of the road and held out her palm. "Hand it over."

He still seemed reluctant to admit defeat. "I can't see the arrows in the dark," he said, as grumpy as an overtired child.

She opened it and handed him two pills. "Do you need help with the water too?"

He said nothing, merely shot her a testy look and unscrewed the cap. He took his dosage and laid his head back, not saying a word.

"Are you warm enough?" The temperature was

dropping and the snow coming down harder as they climbed to a higher elevation. Her wipers and defroster were struggling to keep up.

"I am a little cold," he said grudgingly.

She dug past Murphy in the back and pulled out another blanket, which she spread over Steve's long legs. Much to her surprise, Steve muttered a thank-you.

Tucking the blanket over his wounded shoulder, she took a long look at her patient. Considering the circumstances, she guessed he was doing as well as he could. There was something about him that told her his surliness was only a byproduct of the situation, not a permanent part of his personality.

His dark hair fell over his forehead, and she pushed it back with a light touch. She told herself it was only to check his temperature, but she knew better. She wanted to touch him. Judging by the scars she saw on his face, Steve had certainly seen his share of trouble. Or maybe that was part and parcel of his career, roughing it up with the bad guys. For some reason she was suddenly glad that she was the one who'd found him in the alley. She was the one who could bring him to safety. Wherever that may be.

The falling snow had covered her windshield, creating a cocoonlike atmosphere in the car. Tucked in with Steve, and with Murphy sleeping in the back, she realized how tired she was. Lack of sleep was catching up with her now. And the storm was raging worse than ever. She had no choice but to continue. They'd never ride out the storm on the side of the road.

She pulled back out onto the highway, nearly losing control of her car when her back tires spun out. Gripping the wheel tighter, she slowed, steered into the skid and got control of the car. It had been three years since she'd driven in snow; she'd best remember that.

As she drove down the road toward Rawhide, she debated her options for Steve. If she could keep going until they got to Rawhide, she could take him to the small hospital her brother-in-law and her cousin ran. There would be someone on duty all night long.

But that someone would be a nurse, not Caroline or Jon. There would be talk.

Or she could go straight to Caroline's house. But her husband, Mike, a wonderful man, was also the sheriff for the surrounding area. He would have to report Steve's gunshot wound, according to law.

Jessica decided it might be better to go to her sister's house. Tori was married to Jon, Caroline's partner. Maybe Jessica and Tori could gang up on Jon and convince him to delay reporting the wound for a day or two.

It wasn't as if Steve had done anything wrong. At

least, she hoped not. She'd believed him when he'd said he'd discovered some bad things about his partners and was trying to prove it. Sure, she could have examined the contents of the manila envelope, looking for proof, but he'd trusted her with it, and she didn't want to betray that trust.

It was almost two in the morning when she pulled into the short driveway to her sister's house. She didn't remember to turn off her lights until after they'd hit the house. Jessica hurriedly shut them off and killed the engine, coasting down the drive.

Taking a deep breath, she expelled it slowly, trying to relax after the strain of driving so long. She looked over at Steve, sleeping soundly. She'd need him awake and coherent to get him into the house.

A knock on her side window almost made her jump straight up and bang her head on the ceiling of the car. Her heart slowed down a little when she identified Jon, her brother-in-law, peering in the window.

She unlocked the door and opened it. "Jon! Did I awaken you? I'm sorry."

"No problem. We're both up with Jamie's 2:00 a.m. feeding."

"Oh. Uh, Jon, I...have someone with me."

"You mean Murphy?" Jon asked, but his eyes were searching the darkness in the SUV.

"No. He's a friend."

"Well, wake him up and come on in."

"Okay, but he may need some help."

"Why? Is he sick?"

"Sort of." Jessica turned to her passenger, push-ing against him. "Steve."

"What?" he growled.

"We're at my sister's house. We need to go in-side."

"'Kay."

Jon said, "Should I go around and help him? Does he have the flu?"

"No, he's been shot," Jessica said, knowing she wouldn't be able to keep it secret for long, even if she tried.

"What? Has he seen a doctor?"

"No. I'll explain when we get inside."

"I'm counting on that," Jon said in a determined voice. He circled the vehicle and pulled open the door. "Here, lean on me," he said as Steve slipped from the SUV to the ground.

Murphy, suddenly aroused, jumped into the front and followed Jessica out into the snow. He bounded beside her, seemingly thrilled with the events.

"No, Murphy, we're not going to play. We're go-ing inside," Jessica informed her dog, who seemed to understand because he raced ahead of her to the front door.

Tori was standing at the door, anxiously watching. When Jessica came in, she hugged her sister. "Sorry for disturbing you," Jessica said. "But I didn't know where else to go."

Her sister was already looking past her, to the man her husband was helping to the door. "Who's this?"

"Um, it's Steve," Jessica replied.

"Who is Steve?"

"It's a long story. Oh! I forgot something. I'll be right back." Jessica ran back out to her vehicle and got the manila envelope out from under the driver's seat. If it contained the evidence Steve said it did, she knew he'd want it safely with him.

Back in the house, Jon had put Steve on the sofa and opened his shirt. He was removing the bandage when Jessica got back.

"Does it look bad? I did the best I could."

"Looks like the bullet is still in there. Why didn't you take him to a doctor?" Jon asked sternly.

"Because he refused. He said he was a DEA agent and he had evidence that his partners had gone bad. If I took him to a doctor or called the police, he was sure he'd be killed."

Jon frowned. "You know I have to report the wound, don't you?"

"Yes, but I thought— I hoped maybe you wouldn't have to report it right away. I want him to be able to protect himself."

"First things first. I need to get that bullet out."

"Are you going to take him to the clinic?" Tori asked.

"But you can't!" Jessica protested. "Someone might see him." She moved closer to Steve, wanting to protect him.

"There's only one nurse on duty right now, and I know her well. She doesn't gossip about what happens in the hospital," Jon said.

"You're sure?"

"I'm sure, Jess. But even if I delay telling Mike, that will have to happen. You understand that, don't you?"

She nodded. "Yes, I know. Where can we hide him after you take out the bullet?"

"He'd be safe at the clinic."

"That would cause a lot of talk. Isn't there somewhere I could take care of him and no one would notice?"

"How about Mike's old apartment over the sheriff's office?" Tori suggested. "We could tell everyone Jessica is back, but she wants to stay in town instead of out at the ranch."

Horrified, Jessica said, "We can't tell Mom and Dad that!"

"No, they can be trusted," Tori reassured her. "You know that, Jess."

She did. "Then let's use the apartment. I can take care of him, can't I, Jon?"

"Sure. And if your sister and her husband come see you every once in a while, no one will think anything of it," Jon said as he left the room.

"Where's he going?"

"Probably to get a coat. It's cold outside. Do you have one?"

"Not unpacked. When I left California, it didn't occur to me it would be snowing here," Jessica said with a rueful smile. "Hard to believe I could've forgotten, isn't it?"

"You were gone a long time, sis," Tori said with a smile. "Borrow my coat. I have to stay here with the kids, so I won't need it until morning."

"Thanks, Tori. And do you mind if Murphy stays with you, too?"

Before Tori could answer, Jon came back wearing his coat. He moved to the sofa and shook Steve, who had fallen asleep. "Come on, man. We're going to take that bullet out of you."

"No! No doctors," Steve protested, his voice groggy.

Jon ignored the remark. "Right. Just come with me. It's going to be all right."

"Where is she?" Steve asked.

"Who?"

"The redhead. Where is she?"

Jessica stepped to his side. "I'm here, Steve. It's all right. Jon is going to help you."

"You'll come with me?"

"Yes, I'll be there with you. I promise."

Jon sent a look toward his wife as he helped Steve to his feet.

"Wait!" Jessica called, turning back to get the manila envelope.

"What is that?" Jon asked.

"It's the proof Steve has about his partners' activities. I promised him I'd keep it safe."

"Maybe you should leave that here. I'll put it away."

"I'm afraid someone might've followed us, or will come looking for us tomorrow."

"All the more reason not to take it with you. They won't come here looking for it."

"I don't want to put you in any danger, Tori," Jessica protested.

"I won't be. They won't even know we're kin."

"All they have to do is ask anyone in town."

"Who will send them out to the ranch, not to my house. This way will be safer."

"Okay. Thanks, sis." She hugged Tori and followed Jon and Steve out to her SUV.

Jon helped Steve into the front seat. Jessica could hear Murphy protesting her disappearance. She slipped behind the wheel, hoping to get out of there quickly, so Murphy would settle down.

"I'll follow you to the clinic," Jon said.

Chapter Three

When Jessica parked in back of the clinic, she roused Steve again. "Can you walk if I help you?"

"Where are we?"

"At the hospital in Rawhide. My brother-in-law is going to help you."

"No! I need to get to Washington."

"I'm not even sure I can get you inside, Steve. You can't make it to Washington in your condition."

"My evidence?"

"It's hidden. I'll keep it safe, I promise. Now, I'm going to come to your side and help you out. Pull the blanket around you. It's still snowing."

With that, she slipped out of the SUV, wearing her sister's coat, and opened the door on the passenger side. Steve almost fell into her arms. She braced herself, but fortunately Jon appeared at that moment. "Here, let me help him."

Jessica stepped aside, but she felt a strange sense

of loss. Steve had depended on her for more than twenty-four hours.

She opened the door for the pair and followed them in. Jon turned into the first room and put Steve on a gurney. Then he turned to Jessica. "Stay here with him until I make sure the nurse on duty won't be in the operating room with us. It will just be me, Caroline and Anna."

"You called Caroline? And my mother?" Jessica demanded. "She didn't even know I was coming home."

"I know, but I want her to assist with the surgery. I told your dad to come, too. And Mike. You'll need to explain everything to him. You can trust him to do what's right, Jess. You know that."

"Yes, I know," Jessica admitted with a sigh. "I don't know how I'll explain it to Steve, though."

"Don't try right now. Wait until we get the bullet out and move the two of you into that apartment over the sheriff's office. He'll grasp the obvious then."

"I hope you're right. And I'm glad my parents are coming. I've missed them a lot." And she was glad her mother, who was a nurse-midwife, would be assisting with the surgery.

Jon smiled and patted her on the shoulder. "Welcome home, Jess."

Jessica settled in a chair beside Steve, who appeared to be asleep. She had to have drifted off, too, because in what seemed like a couple of minutes, her mother and father came in and woke her up. After she hugged them, she explained everything.

"You did a dangerous thing, honey," her father, Brett Randall, said. "You could've been killed."

"I know, Dad, but I couldn't just drive away and leave him there to die. You wouldn't have done that."

"Well, no, but—but I'm a man."

"Oh, Dad, you're so hopelessly out of date. Women can be brave, too."

"We're so glad you've come home," Anna said, hugging her again. "Now, I have to go get ready for the surgery. Maybe you should go tell Mike what's going on."

"Yes, as soon as they take Steve into surgery, I'll go to the waiting room. I'm assuming that's where Mike is?"

"He and Caroline had to bring their son, so I think Mike's in there, getting him back to sleep." Anna stretched up and kissed her husband. "I'll see you soon."

Only a few minutes later, Anna came back to take Steve into surgery. Jessica went out to talk to Mike.

She found him and her Dad sitting in the waiting room with cups of coffee. She told him about finding Steve and what he had told her.

"The information he had is in a manila envelope that Tori promised to hold for me. He said it was proof that some of his partners were dirty. And he keeps saying he needs to get to Washington."

"Can we look at what he has?" Mike asked.

"Would it make a difference in reporting his wound?"

"I might be able to hold off for a couple of days," Mike said. "You know, things get mislaid sometimes."

Brett nodded. "That works for me."

"Okay. But we should wait until morning before we call Tori. She should get a little more sleep," Jessica said.

"How about you?" her father asked. "Don't you need some sleep?"

"Yes," Jessica agreed, "but I'll have to wait until I'm sure Steve is all right." She turned back to Mike. "Is it okay if we use the apartment over the sheriff's office? He seems to think these guys will come after him."

"Yeah. I've got the key. You want to run over now and look at it? Maybe unload some of your things?"

"Wait a minute!" her father protested. "I don't want Jess staying there if there's going to be any danger. And she shouldn't be alone with the guy, anyway!"

Jessica was waiting for that response. "Daddy, I'm not your little girl anymore. I'm all grown up."

"Not that grown up!"

"I lived in L.A. by myself. And besides, I promised Steve I'd be beside him all the way."

Mike intervened. "I'm sorry, Brett, but if it's not Jess, than it will have to be Anna."

Her father looked at her as if he'd been caught in a nasty trap.

"I'll be fine, Daddy." She took his silence for approval and turned to Mike. "Let's hurry and get the apartment ready so we can get back before they finish the surgery." Already she felt an odd sensation at being separated from Steve.

She recognized it as loneliness.

IT WAS A LITTLE AFTER FIVE in the morning when Mike and Brett carried Steve up the stairs to the bed Jessica had gotten ready for him.

She stood anxiously at the top of the stairs, knowing Steve was probably in some pain. But she had some pills Caroline had sent to ease his pain, to help him sleep. She would have to start his IV. Thankfully, her mother was following the threesome up the stairs to show her exactly what to do.

When they put Steve in the king-size bed and Jessica pulled the cover over him, she saw him relax. She looked at her mother. "Did they get the bullet out?"

"Yes, and Mike kept it as evidence. Steve is going to be fine. He'll be on an antibiotic drip for three or four days and will need to stay in bed, except for trips to the bathroom. I'll show you how to start the drip."

Jessica drew a deep breath. For a role in Hollywood she'd acted as a nurse, but it hadn't been real. She hoped she could do what was needed.

After watching her mother insert the connection into the needle in his hand, Jessica realized her job would be easy. "Thanks, Mom. How long will it last?"

"I think three hours. An alarm will sound to let you know. If it's not changed at once, it will still be all right. Just do it as soon as possible. We have to keep the antibiotics going to be sure there's no infection."

"Okay. So, it's all right if I sleep in between?"

"Yes, of course, dear. In fact, I can stay and keep an eye on him if you're not comfortable—"

"No! No, I can take care of him."

"We do need you to stay awake until you talk to Tori and tell her to bring that manila envelope to me on her way to work," Mike said. "Can you do that?"

"Yes. Uh, how early does she get up?"

"Jon said she gets up at seven. That's only a couple of hours from now. Then you can sleep all day. I promise I won't do anything until I've looked at the evidence and talked to Steve. Jon and Caroline said he should be able to talk in the morning."

"Thanks, Mike. And you, too, Dad, for getting him here. I'll try to explain everything to him."

"All right, honey, but we wish you'd come home."

"Dad, we've already been through this. I don't want to bring any trouble with me. We'll be fine. And after Steve has settled everything, I'll come home." She hugged her mother and father and Mike, too. Then she watched them go down the stairs.

She was finally alone with Steve again.

Only he was asleep and she wished she was.

Determined to stay awake to talk to Tori, she went into the kitchen and searched for something to eat. Mike had brought some food from his kitchen until the stores opened.

She made herself a cup of hot chocolate and stared out the window at the street below. People rose early in Rawhide, which was quite different from Hollywood.

She wished Murphy was here. Jon had promised to bring him when he came back to the hospital later that day. That would give him an opportunity to check on Steve then, too.

A groan behind her reminded her of Steve's presence. She hurried to his side, feeling his forehead. He was still running a fever. But the antibiotics would take care of that. Maybe it was time for a pain pill.

While getting the pills, she also got a glass of water for him. Then she returned to his bedside. She sat down on the edge of the mattress. "Steve, are you awake?"

He groaned again.

"I have a pain pill here to stop it from hurting. Open your mouth."

He had to have understood because he did as she asked. She raised him so he could drink some water, then settled him back on the pillow. He shivered, and she pulled the blankets closer over his shoulders.

She returned to the window that looked down on the main street of Rawhide. Snow was once again drifting down slowly, adding another layer to the rooftops, streets and the few parked cars.

She'd lived in Rawhide, or near it, almost all her life. From the three years she'd been gone she could see some changes—the café had a new sign; there was a new shop across the street—but basically Rawhide had remained the same. Just the way she liked it. She found a sense of comfort in that sameness.

It was good to be home.

She had to have dozed in a chair by the window, because the ringing telephone woke her at a quarter to seven.

It was Tori. "Jess, are you sure you want me to take this envelope to Mike?"

She explained that Mike might be willing to delay his report, as long as the evidence in the envelope backed up Steve's story. She asked her sister to rush it over to the sheriff's office.

"Will do," Tori replied. "Have you gotten any rest?"

"I'm going to sleep now." The question was where. Surely not on the uncomfortable-looking sofa, not when there was that huge bed that Steve was sleeping in in the other room. She could sleep there and never even touch him.

After Tori promised to bring her some lunch from the café later, Jessica hung up and went to crawl into bed, careful to keep her distance from the patient.

Her last thought was that his body was as good as a furnace.

B.J. RANDALL ANSWERED the phone in the ranch kitchen around ten o'clock. "Hello?"

"Is Jessica Randall there?"

"No, she's not. May I take a message?"

"Well, is this the right place? I mean, this is the number I got from Information. Do you know Jessica?"

"Yes, I do. Who's calling?"

"This is Monica Miller. I'm a friend of Jessica's from L.A."

"I'm her aunt. I can get a message to her if you want."

"Okay. This may be nothing, but a man called this

morning and—and asked for her address in Dallas."
The woman paused. "I know she's from Wyoming.
I said she didn't live in Dallas, she lives in Wyo-
ming."

"Who was the caller?"

"I don't know. I was so taken by surprise I didn't
think to ask. And he wanted to know where in Wyoming, so I told him all I knew was Rawhide. I
hope I didn't cause her any problems. Can you tell
her that?"

"Of course I can. And we appreciate your letting
us know."

After she'd hung up the phone, B.J. dialed the
sheriff's office. "Is Mike in yet?"

"Yes, ma'am. May I tell him who's calling?"

"Yes, it's his mother-in-law."

"Just a minute please."

"B.J., what's up?" Mike asked when he picked up
the phone.

"I'm not sure, but I don't have a good feeling."
She told Mike about the call. "I thought I should let
you know."

"Yeah, I'm glad you did. It confirms what I sus-
pected."

"Does it mean that Jessica is in danger?"

"Possibly. But we're going to keep an eye on her.
And we'll spread the word to keep her location secret. I'm going to make some calls, too."

"We're counting on you, Mike."

"I know, B.J. Jess is family."

THE BANGING ON THE DOOR woke Jessica. She crawled out of the bed and went to unlock the front door after checking to be sure it was her sister.

She was delighted to see that Tori's arms were filled with sacks from the café. "I hope you bought lots of good stuff. I'm starved."

"I did. I even brought some food for you know who. How's he doing?"

"Still sleeping. I changed the drip once."

"Well, maybe we can wake him up after you eat. Oh, and Mike may come up. He said he needed to talk to you."

"Why? Did he read the evidence?"

"I don't know, Jess. He just wanted to know when you'd be awake."

A knock on the door interrupted them. Jessica hurried over and opened the door.

"Did you look before you opened the door?" Mike asked sternly.

"No, but Tori— I thought no one knew where we were?"

"Always check. There've been some developments. Do we still not know Steve's last name?"

"He said he had a driver's license. I haven't looked, but it should be in his pants pocket," she said, waving toward a pile on the end of the sofa. Mike moved to it.

"Go ahead and eat. I know you must be hungry."

She and Tori sat down at the small table. Tori took out the enchiladas and a tossed salad.

"It's enchilada day!" Jessica exclaimed. "I didn't realize that!"

"Some things never change, Jess. I also brought some dessert for you."

"Oh, good."

Mike brought over Steve's driver's license. "This gives his name as Stephen Carter. I'm going to call a friend who used to be DEA. Maybe he'll know the name."

"But it could be an undercover identity," Jessica said, worried.

"I know, but I still need to check. By the way, a friend of yours from Hollywood called. Someone called asking for your home address in Dallas."

Jessica froze. Then she said, "That had to have come from the cop who pulled me over before I left L.A. I told him I was heading home to Dallas, hoping to throw anyone off track."

"Yeah, I remember. You told me that story this morning. I have to admit I thought you were exaggerating but…" He let the thought go unsaid. "Your friend told them it was Wyoming, not Texas. They asked where in Wyoming and she told them Rawhide."

Jessica felt an instant tightness in her chest. "So they'll be here?"

"Maybe. But we're going to be watching out for you. Just don't open the door unless you know who it is."

"I won't, I promise."

"Has he awakened yet?"

"No, Tori and I are going to wake him in a few minutes and try to get him to eat."

"All right. Tell him I haven't reported his wound yet, and I've got his evidence in the safe downstairs. Seems he was right."

"Thank you, Mike. I will."

After Mike had gone and Jessica had eaten, she and Tori went into the bedroom to awaken Steve.

His groggy response wasn't encouraging, but Jessica sat on the side of the bed and got him to take some sips of a chocolate malt. "Maybe this will help his fever go down," she said.

"I have no idea," Tori replied. "It's funny that our mother is a nurse and midwife and neither of us is any good at this medical stuff. Though I have gotten better since I've had kids."

"I hope I have kids," Jessica said in a pensive state, almost as if she didn't realize she was talking aloud.

"Of course you'll have kids. I'm counting on it," Tori said with a laugh. "How else will I have nieces or nephews?"

"I don't know. I was in California for three years, and I never met anyone I was interested in."

"Not even on your last day?" Tori asked.

Jessica stared at her sister. "What are you talking about? Oh, you mean Steve?" She stared at the brown-haired man who had fallen asleep again. She avoided her sister's eyes. "I don't know. Besides, it wouldn't do me any good. I don't live in L.A. anymore."

Tori raised her eyebrows, but she didn't say anything else.

Jessica just smiled and changed the subject as they moved back into the living room. When Tori left for work, Jessica returned to the bedroom.

Once again she tried to rouse Steve and get him to drink more of the chocolate malt. He actually opened his eyes this time, though it was more of a flutter. From what she could see, they were the same color as the malt, a rich chocolate brown.

She couldn't resist the opportunity to talk to him. "Steve, is your last name Carter?"

"Yeah." His eyes closed again, but he mumbled something she couldn't decipher.

She wanted to question him, but there was another knock on the door.

This time she definitely checked and was greatly relieved to find her mother there. "Come in, Mom. I'm glad to see you."

"I hope I'm not keeping you from sleep," Anna said, carefully studying her daughter's face.

"No, I slept about six hours. I may take another nap later, but I'm fine for now."

"And how is our patient?"

"We woke him up and he drank some of a chocolate malt, but he didn't really eat anything. Will that help him?"

"It won't hurt him," Anna said with a smile.

The beeper on his drip sounded. "I'll change it since I'm here," Anna said. "I can check his wound, too."

The two women adjourned to the bedroom. While they were working on the patient, another knock sounded on the door.

"Is that Dad?" Jessica asked.

"No, he had some work he needed to do. Has Mike been here?"

"Yes, when Tori came with my lunch."

"Then who could it be? Make sure you look before you unlock the door."

Her mother didn't need to warn her.

She couldn't get a good look at the person, but she could tell it was a man. Before she had a chance to study him, a booming voice sounded through the door.

"Open this door. I know you're in there."

Chapter Four

Jessica recognized the voice at once. When she'd left Rawhide three years ago, Bobby Daniels had begged her to marry him. But she'd refused.

"Is that Bobby?" Anna whispered.

Jessica nodded and picked up the phone. After dialing a number, she said, "Let me talk to Mike at once, please."

"This is Mike," a strong voice said after a couple of seconds.

"Jess, I'm not going away. Let me in!" Bobby continued to yell.

Jessica ignored him and focused on Mike. "Bobby Daniels is banging on the door, calling my name. He says he knows I'm in here. What do I do?"

"Nothing. I'll take care of it."

She hung up the phone and gestured to her mother to be quiet. A minute later they heard Mike's voice. "Bobby? Come down here please."

"I'm talking to Jess!" Bobby returned, his voice belligerent.

"I'm not going to ask twice. You either get your butt down here or I'll haul you down and throw you in jail!"

Jessica held her breath, waiting for Bobby's response. She let out a sigh of relief when she heard his footsteps going down the stairs.

"How did he know you were here?" Anna asked.

"I don't know but Mike had better find out."

MIKE LED THE RECALCITRANT Bobby Daniels into his office and sat him down. "Now, I want to know who told you Jessica was upstairs."

Refusing to meet his gaze, Bobby said, "I just figured it out."

"Oh, really? You realized Jessica had returned from Hollywood because…"

"Because her mom went up there."

"Right. Since her mom is a nurse, it would be unusual for her to visit anyone but her daughters?"

As if realizing his excuses were not going to satisfy the sheriff, Bobby said, "I heard rumors, okay?"

"Of course. Just a minute." He picked up the phone and dialed two numbers. "Harry, can you come in my office, please?" Then he leaned back in his chair and stared at Bobby, who stirred restlessly in his seat.

"Yeah, Mike?" Harry asked as he came into the office.

"Harry, do you know Bobby Daniels?"

Harry frowned. "We've met."

"Who introduced you?"

"Andy Rivers." He was a deputy on the night shift.

"Oh, that's right. They're close friends, aren't they?" Mike pretended he had no idea of that fact until this minute.

Bobby's cheeks flushed.

"Go call him and tell him I want him here in ten minutes."

"But he'll be sleeping," Harry said.

"Just do as I said," Mike ordered. Then he stood.

Bobby jumped up from his chair. "So I can go?"

"No, I'm afraid not, Bobby. I think you'll be staying with us for a while."

"What do you mean? I didn't break any laws!"

"Sounded to me like you were disturbing the peace with all that yelling."

"Damn it, you can't—"

Mike, who was at least six inches taller and broader in the shoulder, raised an eyebrow. "Are you sure about that?"

"I want a lawyer!"

"Sure. I'll ask Harry to give you your one phone call. You can call the only lawyer in town."

"But he's a Randall!"

"Are you suggesting he won't treat you fairly? I hate to have to tell him you thought that of him."

"No! But— Fine, I'll call him."

Mike took him by the arm and led him to the office door. "Harry, put Bobby in a cell after he calls his lawyer."

"Okay. What are we charging him with?"

"Disturbing the peace," Mike said calmly.

He went back into his office and called upstairs. "Everything's under control, Jess. You did the right thing, calling me. I'm going to post someone across the street with a walkie-talkie, so we won't be taken by surprise again."

After he hung up the phone, he sat there staring at the wall, wishing he didn't have to do what he knew had to be done. It was a shame.

A few minutes later, Andy Rivers knocked on his office door and came in. "Harry said you wanted me, Sheriff?"

"Yes, sit down, Andy."

Mike stared at the young man across from him. Andy had been working as a deputy for a year now. He had potential. But Mike couldn't trust him again.

"I believe before you left this morning I told you about my wife's cousin returning to Rawhide, with the expressed order to not reveal that fact to anyone."

"Yes, sir," Andy said, fear on his face.

"So how do you explain the fact that your best friend knew she was in town and exactly where to find her?"

Andy turned bright red and stared at the floor.

"You've shown promise, Andy, but I have to fire you."

"But, Sheriff—"

"I'm sorry. If you'll drive over to Buffalo and apply there, I'll put in a word for you. That's the best I can do."

After Andy had left his office, Mike stood there, bracing himself on the doorjamb. Then, with a sigh, he looked over his staff. Selecting one of his men, one of the older deputies, he sent him out to the sidewalk across the street to keep an eye on the stairway that led to the apartment upstairs.

"Don't let anyone go up there without reporting it. I'll be the one to decide whether we should take action."

"Yes, sir."

After that, he called Harry into his office again.

"Sir down, Harry. I have a delicate assignment for you."

Harry never hesitated. He was Mike's favorite employee, always responsible, always willing.

"I want you to visit the owners of all the businesses. Tell them kidnappers have threatened Jess. She's gone to ground in Hollywood. But the FBI let us know that the kidnappers might come here, thinking she'd come home. So we need to know if anyone new to town asks about Jess."

"Right."

"I'm going to put men out there at two-hour shifts to keep an eye on the stairs. Can you work up a schedule for me? I've got Macy out there right now."

"Sure. I can do that before I walk around town and spread the word."

"Thanks, Harry."

ANNA WENT TO THE GROCERY store to buy some essentials for Jessica and Steve. Mike had asked that Jessica remain in the upstairs apartment, not show herself around the town.

When Anna returned with Jessica's requests and a few practical things she hadn't thought of, she helped her daughter put the groceries away.

"It's time for me to go, but I don't want to leave you here alone, dear. Will you be very careful?"

"Of course I will, Mom. And I'm not alone. Steve is here with me."

"He can't do much to protect you. He can't even stay awake most of the time," Anna complained.

"I know, but he's getting better, isn't he?" There was a hopeful plea in her voice that alerted Anna.

"Yes. Did you know him before he got shot?"

"No."

"But his recovery seems awfully important to you."

"Of course. I saved him. It's important that he recovers and that he gets the bad guys."

"'The bad guys,' as you call them, could get you. Don't forget that, Jessica."

"I won't, Mom, I promise. And Mike is keeping an eye on us."

"I know. That's the only reason I'm willing to leave you here. I'll be back tomorrow. Your father will probably come with me. He's going to want to meet Steve. When he's awake, I mean."

Jessica locked the door behind her mother and decided to lie down for a nap. She really didn't think Steve's partners would come after him here in Rawhide, but if they did, she trusted Mike to stop them.

Once again she slid into the bed beside Steve and closed her eyes.

Sometime later she heard barking. Immediately coming awake, she recognized those sounds. Murphy had come back to her. She hurried to the door, first looking out the window, to see Jon with her dog.

"Murphy!" she exclaimed as she opened the door.

"Hey, I'm here, too." Jon feigned a pout.

"Hi, Jon," Jessica said. "Come in. I've missed *both* of you."

"Yeah, I could tell whom you missed the most. He's been missing you, too. Our housekeeper said the howling was keeping the baby from sleeping. I thought it was time for him to at least pay you a visit. I think he thought we'd done away with you."

Jessica, who'd been stroking her pet, apologized. "I'm sorry he caused problems."

"It's okay. I'd howl if Tori left me behind," Jon said with a grin. "Now, how's our patient?"

"He's sleeping most of the time."

"I'd better check him out."

They both went into the bedroom.

As Jon checked the wound, Steve woke up. He jerked from Jon's hands, trying to get away.

Jessica soothed him. "It's okay, Steve. You're safe. This is Jon, my brother-in-law."

Slowly, Steve sank into his pillow, taking deep breaths. "You're a doctor?"

"Yes," Jon said as he rebandaged the shoulder.

"How soon can I get up?"

"How do you feel?"

"Weak. But I've got to get out of here. I'm in trouble, and I don't want her to suffer for it."

"Well, let's try a simple trip to the bathroom. While I'm here to help you, it will spare Jessica blushes."

Steve looked at Jessica. "That's your name? Jessica?"

"Yes. I forgot I hadn't told you."

"Come on, Steve," Jon urged. "Let's take our hike to the bathroom."

Steve slid to the edge of the bed and stood up too fast. He almost crumpled, but Jon shored him up.

"Easy there," Jon told him. "It will take a minute to get your legs under you."

Steve steadied himself, then said, "Okay, I'm ready."

After the two men moved in tandem to the bathroom, Jessica stripped the bed and put clean sheets on it. She had just finished when they came out. Hurriedly she turned down the covers.

Steve sank down on the bed, sweat beading on his forehead.

"Jessica, I'm not strong enough to protect you if my partners come after me. I want you to go with Jon, so you'll be safe."

Jessica ignored him, continuing to tuck the covers around him. "Do you need a pain pill?"

"No. Did you hear me?" he asked, grabbing her hand.

"Yes, I heard you."

"Then why are you ignoring me?"

Jon chuckled.

Steve jerked his head around. "What? What's so funny? I promise you it's dangerous for her to stay here."

"I know that. But *you* obviously don't know the Randalls."

"Who are the Randalls?"

Jessica answered that question. "My family. Jon is married to my sister. So even though his last name is Wilson, he's a Randall, too."

"So's Mike," Jon added. At Steve's confused look he added, "The sheriff. You've met him on several occasions."

"Is everyone in this town a Randall?" Steve asked, sounding frustrated.

"Just about," Jon said. "And we're going to take care of you and protect you. And Jessica, too."

"You don't understand how—how desperate these men are. They won't show any mercy!"

"No, I guess not, since their freedom is at stake," Jon agreed.

"Then you understand. Make *her* understand."

Jessica asked, "Then who would take care of you?"

"I'd manage."

"No, you wouldn't!" Jessica exclaimed. "You can hardly get out of bed, and when you do, you're exhausted. You certainly can't cook your meals or dress yourself." She gave him a triumphant look.

He ignored her and looked at Jon. "Tell her those things don't matter. I don't want her to get into trouble because she saved my life!"

"Aha! You admitted it!" she exclaimed.

"Admitted what?"

"That I saved your life!"

"Well, of course I admitted that. It's the truth. If you hadn't picked me up, lied to the policeman, driven almost twenty-four hours straight, I'd be dead by now. I screwed up when I underestimated them." He turned to glare at Jessica. "I'm not making that mistake again!"

Jon intervened. "Neither are we. Mike is a professional from the Chicago P.D. He knows what he's doing, I promise. None of us wants to lose Jess. She's part of the family."

Steve closed his eyes. In a tired voice that told both of his audience he had spent what little energy he had, he muttered, "You don't understand."

Jessica bent down and kissed his brow, as a mother would a sick child, and pulled the cover up a little higher. Then she motioned to Jon to follow her as she tiptoed out of the room.

"He's doing better, isn't he?" she asked anxiously as she moved to the sofa where Murphy waited.

"Yeah, but he's got a ways to go. He should be able to eat a real breakfast in the morning. That will give him some strength. After that he should begin making a rapid recovery."

"Good. Though I'm not sure what will happen then. He thinks he's going to fly to Washington."

"That would take a lot of energy," Jon said doubtfully.

"That's not all it would take. He says his boss is

in on this scheme, too. No doubt they'll be looking for him in Washington if they haven't caught him yet."

"Hmm, think we could get the authorities to come here?"

"I doubt it. Big wigs in D.C. don't do curb service."

"Could someone else deliver the information?" Jon suggested.

"Possibly, but I don't think Steve would go for that. He doesn't want to let the information out of his control until he can turn it over to the head of the DEA."

"We'll have to do some thinking about that," Jon finally said. "I'd best get home. And I'd better take Murphy with me. You couldn't let him outside without showing yourself, and Mike doesn't want that."

"I guess you're right," Jessica said with a sigh. She hugged Murphy's neck and told him to be good for Jon. Jon and the dog went down the stairs, and Jessica locked the door behind them.

Then she went to the kitchen and began cooking supper for her and Steve. She wanted something he could eat easily that would give him energy. She understood that one way or another, they had limited time to resolve Steve's problem.

As she cooked, she considered different solutions. Positive solutions. She refused to consider that Steve, or both of them, might die.

There were two problems. One was surviving the next few days if the bad guys came after them. The second problem was getting to D.C. and into the office of the man in charge of the DEA without being detected.

The ringing phone took her from her thoughts.

"Jess, it's Mike. We found out how Bobby Daniels knew you were there. One of my deputies told him."

"Oh, no! But—"

"Don't worry about it. We're keeping Bobby here for a couple of days. And the deputy has been fired."

"I'm sorry, Mike. That must've been difficult."

"We also spread the word all over town that you're in hiding in Hollywood and we need to know if some stranger asks about you."

"You did? Did anyone say—"

"We just got our first report. A couple of strangers asked after you at the café. The waitress told them all about your Hollywood career and said you hadn't been home for at least six months."

"So did they leave town?"

"Yeah, they went to Buffalo to get a hotel room, but I doubt that's the last of them."

"Okay. So we just stay inside and wait?"

"Afraid so, Jess. You making it all right?"

"Yes. I'm just about to give Steve some dinner."

"Good. Caroline and I may pay you a visit after dinner. Will that be all right?"

"I'd love for you to come. Maybe Steve will be able to stay awake for a little while and the two of you can talk."

"That would be good."

After she hung up the phone, Jessica finished cooking. When the stew was ready, she carried a bowl of it in to Steve.

"Wake up, Steve. I've got some dinner for you," she announced as she sat down on the edge of the bed.

When he didn't respond, she put the bowl on the bedside table and shook him. "Steve? You need to wake up so you can eat dinner."

"Okay," he mumbled.

"Come on, open your eyes."

One brown eye appeared. Then the other one. "Yeah? What do you want?"

"I'm trying to feed you supper," Jessica assured her patient. She reached for the bowl and filled the spoon. "Open up," she ordered.

"Mmm, that's good," Steve muttered, surprise on his face. "I didn't know you could cook."

"Red made sure we all could cook, even the guys."

"Who is Red?"

"He's like our grandfather," Jessica told him.

"Like? What do you mean?"

"He raised my dad and his brothers. He's not

blood-related, but we all love him." She put another spoonful of stew in his mouth.

After five spoonfuls, Steve sank back against his pillow. "That's enough."

Jessica didn't accept his decision. "The more you eat, the sooner you'll be strong enough to leave here."

Steve frowned. "Okay."

"More stew?"

"Yeah, sure," he said, and struggled to hold his head up.

"Just lay back. I can feed you without you lifting up your head."

After several more bites, Steve asked, "Has there been any sign of my former partners?"

Jessica waited until she'd fed him the next bite. Then she said, "Maybe."

He reached up and held her arm to stop her feeding him. "What do you mean?"

"There were some men asking about me at the café."

"Maybe they were old friends?"

"No. They weren't."

"Where are they now?"

"Mike said they went to Buffalo for the night."

"Who's Mike?" Steve snapped.

Jessica sighed. "I thought Jon told you this afternoon. Mike is the sheriff and Caroline's husband."

"And who is Caroline?"

"She's my cousin and she assisted Jon with your surgery. They're coming to see us in a little while."

"Why?"

With an exasperated sigh, Jessica said, "He wants to talk to you. And Caroline can check your wound to be sure it's healing all right."

His hand dropped from her arm and she continued to feed him.

Finally, he told her he couldn't eat any more stew.

Jessica didn't press him this time. "Okay. You did a good job. Why don't you take a nap, and I'll wake you up when Mike and Caro get here."

His only answer was a grunt as he closed his eyes.

Jessica sat quietly, watching him as his breathing deepened and the frown on his brow slowly disappeared. With tenderness, she smoothed his dark brown hair from his brow. He was a big man, like the men in her family. And, like them, he was very handsome. Once again she was overcome by the desire to touch him, like in the car. That time she'd allowed her hands and eyes to make contact with him. But now she reined in her errant hand. The situation was different. They were alone in an apartment; Steve was mending. Touching him, she knew, wouldn't be smart.

Finally, she abandoned his bedside and went to the kitchen to eat her own bowl of stew. She'd forgotten how good a hot meal felt when it was cold outside. The only times she had gotten cold in Hollywood were when the air conditioning was set too low.

As she sat at the table, thinking about the changes she was making in her life, she heard footsteps on the stairway. Thinking Mike and Caroline had arrived, she hurried to the door. But she didn't open it, waiting until they identified themselves.

Only no one spoke.

Chapter Five

Suddenly, a loud whistle rent the air, followed by heavy footsteps racing down the stairs.

Jessica ran to the window that overlooked the street. She saw the backs of two men as they raced to an SUV parked by itself halfway down the street. She heard shouting. Then there were footsteps coming up the stairs, lighter but noticeable. She watched Mike run down the street, so she guessed her visitor was Caroline.

"Jess? Are you all right?" Caroline called before Jessica could get to the door. She swung it open and fell into Caroline's embrace.

"Yes, I'm fine. I realized someone was out there, but I thought it was you and Mike. When no one spoke, I was frightened."

"With good reason. Someone was supposed to be watching the stairs. Mike's going to raise a ruckus with whoever was on guard. It'll be a few minutes before he gets here."

"That's all right."

"Jessica?" Steve called from the bedroom.

Walking toward the bedroom, she said, "Excuse me, Caroline. I'm sure I worried Steve when I ran out of the room." She entered his room and reassured him. "Everything's fine, Steve. Sorry I woke you."

"Why did you run out?"

"I, um, well, I heard someone on the stairs and figured it was Caroline. And it was." No way was she telling him about the two men.

"Is Mike with her?"

Before Jessica could answer, Caroline joined them and said, "He'll be here a little later." She stepped to the bed. "May I go ahead and look at your wound?"

Steve was watching Jessica, but he nodded to Caroline. While she undid the bandage, he said to Jessica, "What are you not telling me?"

Jessica's head jerked up and she met Steve's stare. "Uh, I didn't— I mean, I don't want you to worry."

Steve winced as Caroline touched his wound. But his words were directed toward Jessica. "Did they come?"

"Who?"

"Jess, you should tell him the truth," Caroline said as she put on a new bandage and checked the drip.

Steve stared at her, waiting for her to speak.

"I—I think one of the men was at the door. Maybe he was trying to listen in, but you were asleep, and I wasn't talking. I thought it was Mike and Caroline, but whoever it was didn't say anything. Then I heard a loud whistle and steps running down the stairs. That's when I came in here to look out the window. I saw two men running down the sidewalk and jumping in an SUV. Mike chased after them."

"What did they look like?" Steve demanded, his voice tight.

"I only saw them from the back, Steve," Jessica explained.

"Close your eyes and watch them running away. Then tell me what you see."

Though she didn't think that would help, Jessica couldn't resist Steve's compelling stare. Closing her eyes, she tried to picture the two men running away. Surprisingly a mental picture formed. With her eyes still closed, she said, "One was taller than the other—and leaner. They were both white and dressed in jeans."

"Marcus and Baldwin," Steve muttered. Then he struggled to sit up. "I've got to get out of here!"

"Whoa!" Caroline exclaimed and gently pushed Steve back to the pillow. "Where do you think you're going?"

"If I don't get out of here, I'm going to get Jessica killed," he told Caroline. Since she was blocking his way, he tried to roll to the other side of the bed.

Jessica watched him, saying nothing. She figured he'd realize his problem sooner or later.

"Hey! Where are my clothes?" he demanded, proving her right.

"Not here," she said cheerfully. "Guess you'll have to stay a while."

"Jess, I'm not kidding. They'll be back, and I don't think I can protect you!"

"Wait until Mike gets here," Caroline urged. "He'll protect you both."

Steve ignored her. "Jess, I need my clothes!"

Jessica shook her head. "It's cold out there. Even if you had your clothes, it wouldn't be enough. Besides, you're wounded."

"I know I am, but—"

All three of them froze as they heard more footsteps. Then Caroline said, "I'm sure that's Mike."

"Stay in here with Steve," Jessica ordered. Then she left the room to go to the front door. "Who is it?"

"It's Mike."

She recognized his voice and opened the door. "Did they get away?"

He looked disgusted. "Yeah. Are you and Steve okay?"

"We're both fine. Come on in." She led the way to the bedroom.

Mike hugged his wife, then turned to Steve.

"You had two visitors tonight. I didn't catch them, but I suspect they were—"

Steve interrupted him. "My partners, Marcus and Baldwin! Jessica saw them and described them."

Mike looked at Jessica. "You saw them?"

"Just from the back. I ran in here and looked out that window and saw them running away." Jessica looked at Steve. "He said their names. I guess he recognized them by my description."

"So these men were your partners in L.A.?" Mike asked Steve.

"Yeah. Can you get me some clothes? I need to get out of here. They're after me, and they're not going to go away until I do."

"Leaving won't protect Jessica until you announce your departure, and that wouldn't be smart." Mike looked at his wife. "How's his wound?"

"Healing nicely," Caroline said. "He should be off the antibiotic in another twenty-four hours. It'll take him a few days to regain his strength, but he'll be as good as new."

"Where are the clothes we brought him?" Mike asked. That question got Steve's attention. "You brought me clothes? Then I can get out of here!"

"No, Steve," Mike said at once. "We brought you clothes to preserve your modesty, that's all. I thought I'd help you get dressed while I'm here."

"He can probably use a trip to the bathroom, too," Jessica added.

As Caroline came back into the room, a small stack of clothes in her hand, Mike asked her, "Can he take a shower?"

"I suppose so, but I just redid his bandage." She looked at first Mike and then Steve. "Okay, go ahead. I'll redo it when he gets out."

"Thanks," Steve muttered.

Jessica and Caroline went into the living room, since all Steve wore was his underwear.

"As soon as Mike gets him into the bathroom, we should remake the bed," Caroline said.

"I don't think there are any more clean sheets," Jessica said, frowning.

"I brought some clean sheets in the bag with his clothes. I figured you'd be needing some. We can take your laundry home with us and wash it for you."

"Thanks, Caro. You're the best."

As they made the bed, Jessica thought aloud. "Now that Steve's getting better, I need a plan to keep him here."

"Jess, what are you talking about? You can't keep him here. He's not a prize or…a puppy you brought home."

"I know that, but I feel responsible for his safety. After all, I brought him here," Jessica said, an unspoken plea in her voice.

"If you hadn't, he would've died. This situation isn't your fault," Caroline assured her.

"I know that, but how is he going to escape and make it to Washington by himself?"

"I don't see how you can help him," Caroline returned.

"Now that he's awake more, we can make a plan."

"Your daddy's not going to let you put yourself in danger any more than he can help it. You know that."

"But, Caro—" Her response was cut short when the bathroom door opened and the men emerged, Mike helping Steve walk to his bed. His chest was still bare, giving Jessica a broad view of his wound for the first time. She drew in a sharp breath.

"We thought you should rebandage him before I help him with the T-shirt," Mike said.

"Yes, of course," Caroline agreed.

Jessica hurriedly turned down the covers. "We changed the sheets again."

"Thanks," Steve said, but it sounded more like a grunt. It was clear that the shower and trip to the bath had taken a lot out of him.

With Mike's help, he slid his legs under the cover and lay back on the pillows Jessica had piled up.

"This won't take long," Caroline assured him. She quickly bandaged him and then reinserted the drip after Mike helped him put on a T-shirt. "There. How do you feel?"

"The shower helped a lot…and the clothes. Thank you both," Steve said, actually managing a weak grin.

Caroline looked at Jessica. "I think a cup of hot chocolate might be appropriate right now. And Mike and I could use some coffee."

"Oh, yes, of course." Jessica jumped up and started for the kitchen.

"I'll be right there to help you," Caroline called after her. Then, she turned to her husband. "Jessica feels responsible for him, Mike. You've got to find a way to keep her safe," she said in a whisper. Then she hurried out of the room.

"She's not responsible," Steve protested.

"You know that, and so do I," Mike assured him. "Jessica, however, is another matter. She's always been hardheaded, according to Caroline. Her parents weren't happy about her running off to Hollywood, but they couldn't stop her."

Steve frowned ferociously. "You've got to do something. Take her downstairs and lock her up."

"Stubbornness is not a reason to get arrested."

"Don't you see? That's why I have to leave. I'll lead the guys away from here." Steve pleaded with the sheriff one more time. "Can't you get me some shoes and a coat?"

Mike leaned against the wall. "Well, I could, but that would kind of put me between a rock and a hard place."

"What do you mean?"

"Your doctor said it's too early for you to go, and she's my wife, and Jessica would be furious, and she's my wife's cousin."

"How about the other doctor? I can't remember his name."

"That would be Jon Wilson. But he's married to Jessica's sister."

"Oh." Steve collapsed against the pillows again. "What am I going to do?"

"Is there anyone you'd trust to take the evidence to the DEA for you?"

"No! My boss there is part of the group profiting from the sales of confiscated drugs. I don't know if it goes any farther up the chain, but I'd like to take it to the head of the DEA, just to be sure. And I can't ask anyone else to put themselves in danger."

"So we have to find a way to get you safely out of here and into the DEA building," Mike said slowly, rubbing his chin.

"What are you talking about?" Jessica asked sharply as she came through the door, carrying a steaming mug. She turned to Steve. "Here's your hot chocolate. Do you need help sitting up more?"

"No." He tried to raise himself up to a sitting position, but he collapsed against the pillows with a groan.

Mike stepped forward. "Relax, I'll help you," he

said and slipped his hands under Steve to help him sit up.

Jessica handed the cup to Steve and asked her question again. "What were you two discussing?"

Mike spoke up. "Uh, we were discussing how Steve should get his evidence to D.C."

"And did you come up with any ideas?"

He shook his head. "I'm afraid not. We can handle getting him out of town okay, but getting him to the office of the head of the DEA would be pretty difficult."

Jessica narrowed her eyes. "Unless someone knew the head of the DEA." After a moment, she said, "Maybe my dad knows him, or knows someone who does."

Steve shook his head. "I'd have to go in unarmed, and I'd be killed before I even got to his office. Miguel would have every agent and officer gunning for me, telling them I was the dirty one.

"He's second in command at the DEA—Miguel Antonio, my boss. He's in this up to his eyeballs, I'm sure of it. I've just got to get the proof on him. Either way, he'd never let me in alive."

"Yeah, you're right," Mike agreed. He turned to Jessica. "How would Brett know someone at the DEA?"

"Dad used to spend time in D.C., talking to the senators about conservation and grazing rights on park lands. He doesn't go to Washington much anymore, but he still knows people there."

"I didn't know that," Mike said. "Then maybe he does know someone there who could get Steve in."

"And you could wear a disguise so you wouldn't be recognized," Jessica interjected.

"I think Halloween's already been celebrated, honey," Steve said with a wry smile. "Besides, people don't often trick-or-treat at the DEA."

"I didn't mean that kind of disguise. I've been living in Hollywood. They use disguises all the time."

"But we're not making a movie," Steve said.

Jessica got a stubborn look on her face.

Caroline, who had followed her in with cups of coffee for her and her husband, said, "I think you should drink your chocolate while it's still hot."

Steve shot her a grateful look.

"I'm not giving up on my idea," Jessica said, glaring at Steve.

"He's not going anywhere yet," Mike assured Jessica. "We've got time to do some thinking. When is your dad coming to see you?"

"Tomorrow, with Mom."

"Oh, yes, Anna said for you to make a grocery list and she'd do some shopping before she came," Caroline said.

"Okay. Maybe we should go into the living room and let Steve get some rest."

"I'll stay with him until he finishes his drink," Mike promised.

Jessica didn't look convinced, but followed Caroline into the living room. "I meant what I said about a disguise. I'm sure I could make him look different enough to fool those men."

"Well, you have a couple of days, at least, to think about it. But don't be surprised if he doesn't accept it," Caroline warned. "After all, his life depends on it."

"I know."

Jessica sat down to make a grocery list, but all she could think of was her plan.

A couple of minutes later, Mike came into the living room, pulling the door closed behind him. "I think he'll be asleep in about a minute. We wore him out this evening."

"I'm sure we did," Caroline agreed. "As soon as Jessica finishes her list, we can go home and rest, too."

"I can call Mom in the morning and tell her what I need. You don't have to wait. But I did want to ask you, Mike, what happened to your deputy watching the stairs?"

Mike's expression turned angry. "He went for a bathroom break. I put someone else on the job. But I want you to leave the outside light on all night. The shadows make it hard to determine if someone is on the stairs."

"No problem. But I have another question. I had a permit for the gun my dad gave me here in Wyoming. When I moved to California, I applied for a gun permit there. Is my Wyoming permit still good?"

Mike shook his head. "Jess, I don't think—"

"I don't want to be here with no protection if those men get past your deputy again, Mike!"

"She has a point, honey," Caroline said.

"I know. Yeah, you're covered," Mike said. "But if you think someone is out there, don't stand in front of the door. They'll fire right through the wood. If you have any doubts at all, don't come into the room until they stop firing. As soon as you see either man try to enter, fire on them. Have you practiced?"

"Yes, I went out every couple of weeks to a gun club and did target practice. Dad made me promise."

"Where's your weapon?"

"Here, in my suitcase." Jessica walked over to the suitcase she had left open on the floor, not bothering to unpack. She picked up the gun, checked it and then handed it to Mike. "It's unloaded."

"Do you have ammo for it?"

"Of course. But I didn't want to load it until I'd cleared it with you."

"All right. Go ahead and load it and put it where you can get to it quickly. If they try to come in, you won't have much time. But, Jess, I've got a good man watching. I don't think they'll try it again to-night."

"I'm sure you're right, Mike. I just want to be pre-pared."

"You could give the gun to Steve and hide on the other side of the bed," Mike suggested, a worried look on his face.

Caroline and Jessica exchanged a look.

"Come on, honey. We need to go home now. Jessica knows what to do."

"Yeah, but I'm afraid Brett won't be happy with me."

"He'll only be unhappy if something happens to Jessica. You just said they wouldn't try anything again tonight. You can talk to Brett tomorrow, and maybe he'll have some ideas."

"I already know his idea. He wants them to move out to the ranch, but I don't think that's wise," Mike said, still frowning.

"I don't either," Jessica agreed.

It was one thing for her to put herself in danger, but she would never, ever endanger the one thing she treasured most—her family.

Chapter Six

Jessica curled up on the sofa to think out a plan to rescue Steve again. All her life, her family had teased her about her flair for the dramatic, her fantasizing, her pretending. She'd proved them wrong about those things being useless. After all, she'd actually had some success in Hollywood.

Besides, she thought, it was those very skills that might save Steve now.

With her eyes closed, she daydreamed different scenarios. The one constant in each of them was her presence. She wasn't going to stay home and knit! Women could handle more difficult things these days. And she'd convince her father and Steve that that was true.

Several hours later, without having pinned down a plan, Jessica gave up and got ready for bed. She took a shower and dressed in warm-up pants and a T-shirt, like Steve. Then she crept around the bed and pulled back the covers.

When she sat down, the motion had to have awakened Steve. He grunted and tried to raise up.

"It's okay, Steve. It's just me. Go back to sleep."

He had to have recognized her voice because he settled back down.

After she slid under the covers and relaxed a discreet distance from Steve, knowing her parents still wouldn't approve, she sighed and closed her eyes.

They popped open wide as a strong arm reached out and pulled her close to his big, warm body.

Steve never opened his eyes.

Jessica found herself fighting the desire to snuggle up against him, feeling safe and protected, like some heroine in a movie where the hero always saved her.

But things weren't going to go like that, she reminded herself. She was going to participate in this dangerous situation.

But for tonight, just for tonight, she scooted just a little bit closer to that warm body. Just for tonight.

THE RINGING PHONE WOKE Jessica the next morning.

Unfortunately, it also awakened Steve.

"What are you doing?" he demanded in a gruff, sexy voice.

"Answering the phone," Jessica said as she scrambled from the bed, since the only phone was in the living room. She was grateful that she didn't have to face Steve until she'd regained her distance.

"IS ANYONE FOLLOWING US?" Marcus asked as he drove the SUV down the dark Wyoming highway.

His partner looked over his shoulder. "Can't see anyone. Back in Rawhide, did you see Steve at that apartment? Is that where he is?"

"I didn't see him. Or hear anything, until you whistled. Then I saw that big man coming after me and hauled ass." He shot his partner, Baldwin, a look. "You almost passed me heading for the car."

"I didn't want to try explaining my behavior to him," Baldwin explained.

"Me neither. But I'd bet that's where Steve is. I don't think he could be in very good shape, either. Not after I plugged him in that alley."

"It doesn't take a lot of muscle to pull a trigger. And I'm not interested in sacrificing myself for Miguel's sake. He sure wouldn't do it for us."

"Maybe not," Marcus said, "but if Steve gets to D.C. with the proof Miguel says he has, none of us will be able to defend ourselves."

Baldwin gave a big sigh. "I know. But I don't like the thought of killing Steve."

"Me neither, but I like even less the possibility of losing our gravy train. My wife's gotten used to it, I can tell you."

"Haven't you put enough away in an offshore account? We could cut and run today and be all right for a long time."

Flicking his gaze to the rearview mirror, Marcus slowed his speed around a mountain curve. "Maybe, unless Miguel found us. And you know he'd come after us, don't you? As long as he drew breath he wouldn't let us live."

Baldwin breathed out deeply. "So we've got no choice."

"Right," Marcus said on a deep-throated grunt. "And you'd better not forget it, or I'll come after you, too. Right after I get Steve Carter."

"DARLING, IT'S MOM. You didn't call in your grocery list last night like you told Caroline you would."

"Sorry, Mom. I was busy trying to figure out how to help Steve."

"I see. Well, is there anything you need?"

"Yes, Mom, uh, let me think."

"Did I wake you up?" Anna asked.

"Yes, you did, but that's my fault. I stayed up too late and just overslept."

After she gave her mother a hastily concocted list, Anna asked, "How is the patient this morning?"

"I haven't checked on him yet. But I'm going to make his breakfast and feed him. Since he's been eating, he's getting stronger."

"Yes, of course. I'll check him when I get there. Is there anything he needs?"

"Well, Caroline and Mike brought him some warm-up pants and a T-shirt, but it might be nice if he had a change of clothing."

"Of course. He's about your dad's size, isn't he?"

"Yes. He's very tall and lean and— Well, you know."

"Yes, dear, I know. I thought your father and I would join you for lunch so we can get to know the young man. Red is already cooking. He insisted."

Jessica couldn't hold back a smile. "Give him and Mildred my love. I'll be out to see them as soon as possible."

"I will. We'll be there around noon."

BRETT LOOKED UP AS HIS wife hung up the phone and returned to her seat at the kitchen table.

"Everything all right?" he asked.

"Yes, I suppose so."

"You don't sound like it," Brett said, putting his arm on the back of her chair. "What's our daughter number two done now?"

"Do you remember when we first met?"

Jake Randall, who was sitting with them, laughed. "You mean when you threw him on the floor?"

"Sort of. There was an instant attraction, even if we both denied it."

"You're right about that," Brett agreed. "It took me awhile to realize it, though. Hey! You never told me that. You knew at once?"

"Pretty much, though I didn't think it would happen. After all, you were engaged," she pointed out with a grin.

"It didn't take him all that long to dump her once he met you," Jake reminded her. "Why did you bring that up?"

Anna shot her husband a look before she said, "I detected that same feeling in Jess's voice."

"About that DEA agent?" Brett roared. "No! No, that's impossible! I'm not having my little girl go back to that city of sin!"

"When's the last time you were able to tell Jess what to do?" his brother Jake asked him.

Brett glared at Jake. "She listens to me!"

B.J., Jake's wife, entered the kitchen. "What's all the yelling about?"

Red, who was at the stove, checking on something in the oven, said, "Brett is laying down the law about Jess. But I didn't hear what she did wrong. She came home, didn't she?"

"She hasn't been here yet!" Brett pointed out. "And Anna says she's got a thing for this guy who's causing all the trouble."

"It's not his fault, is it?" Red muttered.

Before Brett could respond to Red's words, Anna

said, "I'm not saying they're getting married. I'm just saying when we visit them today, you might try to learn something about him, about his plans for the future. I don't want Jess going back to California any more than you do."

"Has Tori met him?" Brett asked suddenly.

"No, I don't think so."

"Tori's levelheaded, not like Jess."

B.J. looked at Brett. "Shame on you. Jess is different, but that doesn't make her a flake."

Brett buried his head in his hands. Then he raised his head and sighed. "You're right, but I've been so worried about her out in L.A."

"A' course you have," Red said, leaving the stove to come put a grizzled hand on Brett's shoulder. "That's the way it is for parents. I sure worried enough about you scalawags."

"Hey, we were good!" Jake exclaimed.

Red shot him a grim smile. "Right. You never got in fights or caused trouble. Your teachers loved having a Randall in their classes. Except maybe Brett in math classes. He did good. But the rest of you just caused trouble."

"Aw, Red," Jake protested, "we weren't that bad."

"No, I guess not. But don't you fuss at Jessie. She's just a little girl."

Anna chuckled. "You always were soft on the

girls, Red. But Jess will tell you she's all grown up, you know."

"Yeah, but it's hard to forget that redheaded little sprite trying to keep up with the boys. She didn't ever back down," Red said with a fond smile.

"She's not backing down now, either. She saved this man's life…and she wants to keep protecting him." Anna looked at her husband. "Just be prepared. She's trying to work out an escape plan."

"Okay, honey," Brett agreed with a sigh. "You win. We'll just have to figure something out that won't put her or him in danger."

JESSICA DECIDED SHE DIDN'T want to face Steve without something to distract him, so she began preparing breakfast. She took out a tray and loaded it with food and a cup of hot chocolate.

Then she took it to the bedroom door, pausing to balance the tray against the wall while she opened the door. She entered the room and lifted her gaze to face Steve for the first time that day.

He wasn't there.

The panic that filled her was a bad sign. Taking a calming breath, she noted that all the windows were still closed. But the door to the bathroom was also closed.

"Steve?"

"Yeah, I'll be out in a minute."

With a sigh of relief, she put the tray down on the bed and moved to the bathroom door. When it finally opened, she turned to smile at him. "Need some help to get across the room?"

"No," Steve said in a stern voice. "I can make it. But we need to talk."

Steve saw Jessica duck her head. Clearly, she didn't want to answer his question any more than he wanted to ask it. This young woman had saved his life. But he couldn't allow her to make this a romantic thing.

Hell, he didn't even know if he'd survive the week.

"Let's go to the table for breakfast," he said.

"Are you sure…" She looked at him and gulped. "Okay." She turned and picked up the tray off the bed. Then she headed toward the breakfast table. Once she got there, she put the dishes on the table and sat down. She didn't offer to help him.

Steve collapsed in the chair, grateful he didn't have to take another step. After his breathing slowed, he looked at Jessica Randall. The woman who'd saved his life.

"Jess, why were you in bed with me this morning?"

To his surprise, she didn't look embarrassed or apologize. Instead, she raised one eyebrow. "Did you expect me to sleep on the floor? It's a king-size bed, Steve, and we were both dressed."

"But when we woke up——"

She shrugged. "I'm not going to apologize for what I did while I slept…or what you did, either. Eat your breakfast while it's hot. Mom and Dad are coming to have lunch with us."

Steve stared at her. "Why?"

She sighed in exasperation. "Because they miss me. Is that so hard for you to understand?"

"No, but sometimes fathers want to protect their daughters. I think you should go home with them."

Jessica picked up her coffee cup and took a sip before she answered. "You're being ridiculous, Steve. I'm not going anywhere until you're ready to go."

"I can leave today."

"No, you can't. You're not strong enough yet. And we don't have a plan."

"What do you mean 'we'?" Steve was getting a bad feeling in his stomach. He didn't need the responsibility of Jessica's safety on his back along with everything else.

"I'm thinking of how to get you into the DEA director's office."

"Don't think about it, Jessica. This isn't some TV show. It's life or death."

"Do you think I don't realize that?" she exclaimed, standing up and pacing about the room. "Do you think I didn't notice the bleeding when I put you in my truck? It's a wonder they didn't kill me then, too. I've already risked my life for you. So don't you dare try to tell me I don't realize how serious this is!" She ended up in front of him with her hands on her hips.

"Calm down, Jess," he said, rising with some difficulty. "I didn't mean—"

"Yes, you did! You were ready to pat me on the head and send me home! Well, you can't do that, so don't think you can!"

"Whew!" Steve said as he collapsed in his chair. "You came by that red hair honestly, didn't you?"

"And what is that supposed to mean?"

"You know, red hair, temper. They go hand in hand, don't they?"

"Didn't you meet my mom?"

"I don't know. Did I?"

"She was here. She's a redhead and she doesn't have a temper. She's the most patient person I know," Jessica said.

He heard something in her voice. "Hard to live up to, huh?"

"Yes," Jessica admitted. "Yes, she is. I'm lucky to have her for a mother."

"Did you throw temper tantrums as a kid?" he asked with a wry grin. It was easy to picture a little redheaded girl stomping her foot, expecting the world to conform to her demands.

"Just once or twice. Dad yelled at me, and Mom took me aside and pointed out the problems with losing control. None of the other kids were like me."

"Other kids? How many were there in your family?"

"Oh, I think there were ten or eleven of us. I lose count," she said with a smile.

"Your poor mother!"

"No, they weren't all her kids."

"So your father was married twice?" he asked.

She shook her head. "I should explain. My dad and his three brothers inherited the ranch, and none of them intended to marry after Uncle Jake had a nasty divorce. Then Uncle Jake—he's the oldest—started matchmaking, so they'd have children to leave the ranch to. After he was successful, his sisters-in-law turned the tables on him. And they all lived together on the ranch."

Steve stared at her. "When you were a little girl, you lived with all your cousins on a ranch?"

"Yes. And during the summers, the four brothers would take us camping up in the mountains."

"Your mother didn't go?"

Jessica laughed. "No, she considered that her vacation. The four mothers usually went to Cheyenne shopping."

Steve watched Jessica's face light up with joy as she talked about her family. He wished he'd had such fond memories. But his mother had been a druggie. That was why he had this job. Trying to shut down the disease that drove mothers to prostitution and to abandon their children.

"Your childhood sounds perfect," he said with a wry smile.

She sank down in the chair next to him. "What was your childhood like?"

He shrugged and started eating his breakfast to avoid answering questions. "This is good."

"Thanks."

"Aren't you having any?"

"Yes. I wanted to wait and see how much you ate this morning. I'll finish what's left or cook some more."

Steve immediately put some of his scrambled eggs and bacon on her plate. "Eat while it's still warm."

She picked up her fork and began to eat. He passed her the biscuits and she took one. After she bit into it, she sighed. "I've never learned to make biscuits like Red. His are much lighter."

"Honey, I'd rather have yours any day of the week," he said with a warm smile. Then he stiffened. "I mean, I'm not used to biscuits as good as these. If they were better, I wouldn't know what to do."

"I liked your first response better. Why did you change?"

"Because I was flirting, and I didn't mean to."

"Why not?"

Steve sighed. Resisting temptation was a way of life for him, but it seemed more difficult this morning, sitting at the breakfast table with a great breakfast and an even greater woman. He'd dreamed of a woman he could love and build a good life with. But his dream woman had never been as vibrant or sweet as Jessica.

"Jess, you know why not. Two men are trying to kill me. If they don't succeed, my boss in D.C. will do the job. We're not children playing in the school yard. We have to face facts."

Jessica put down her fork. "I know that. But I don't intend to live my life with fear. And I don't think you should either."

Steve glared at her. "I'm not!"

"If this were your last week," she said slowly, "wouldn't you want to experience the best in life?"

Steve got up from the table and started for the bedroom, though he wasn't moving very fast.

It didn't take incredible speed for Jessica to get in front of him. "Where are you going?" she demanded.

"Back to bed. I've got to rest so I can get out of here before you drive me crazy!" he exclaimed. He'd finally realized Jessica would be hard to deter.

"Drive you crazy?" she repeated, upset. "I'm not doing anything to drive you crazy."

"Honey, just standing there looking like you do is enough to drive me crazy. You're the kind of woman who needs promises and a future. I can't give you any of those things!" He was disturbed about how quickly they'd progressed to deep water.

"I never asked for promises." Her quiet voice shook him.

"Jess, please, I can't— I need to rest." He hated using his physical condition, but he didn't think he was strong enough to resist her sweetness if he didn't.

She took his arm to help him back to the bed. After she got him settled, she asked, "Is there anything I can get you?"

Her voice was stilted and he knew he'd hurt her feelings, but he had no choice. Maybe, if he survived this week, he could make some changes in his life and make a new start that would include a bright star like Jessica. A star that would warm him and fill him with joy all the days of his life.

But not now. "No, thanks, I'm fine. I'm just going to sleep for a while."

JESSICA CLOSED THE DOOR to the bedroom and began clearing the table. She thought better when her hands were busy. And she had a lot to think about.

She'd never felt this way about a man. It was a strange feeling, too. A sense of possessiveness, fascination and vulnerability.

For a man who thought he had no future.

What was she going to do now?

She had no idea. And no one to ask. Except her sister. Tori had always been there for Jessica, even when she hadn't wanted her to be.

That was what she'd do. She'd call Tori after her parents left. And admit that she was confused about her feelings for a man who didn't want her.

Chapter Seven

Jessica hugged both her parents, delighted to see them.

Her father hugged her tighter. "I'm so glad you're home," he whispered.

"Me, too," she returned, fighting the tears that filled her eyes.

Anna had continued on to the kitchen and was now unpacking a picnic basket.

Jessica hurried over. "What did Red make for lunch?"

"Your favorite, of course," Anna returned. "Chicken spaghetti, along with a salad and some green beans. He felt a hearty meal would make your friend get well faster."

"I'm not sure that would be a good thing," Jessica said, hanging her head.

"Why not?" Brett demanded.

"Because he'll try to leave, and we don't have a plan to protect him yet."

He raised his eyebrows. "We?"

Jessica straightened her back and raised her chin, sending a determined look toward her father.

He lifted both hands. "Whoa! I didn't mean— Okay, I did. I don't see how you're involved in protecting this guy. You've already saved his life. What more do you have to do?"

"I feel responsible for him. And—and I don't want him to die!" Jessica exclaimed.

Her mother abandoned the food and put her arms around her daughter. "We don't want that either, dear, but we don't want you to be hurt."

"That's why I'm trying to come up with a good plan, so we all get what we want. Dad, do you know anyone in Washington who might know the head of the DEA?"

Brett frowned. "Maybe. Why?"

"I've been thinking. We have to have an innocent reason for Steve to go to that building. What if he were a tourist and his senator or representative got him an appointment with the head of the DEA?"

"That request would be unusual…but not impossible," Brett agreed. "But wouldn't he be recognized?"

"That's where my skills come in to play. In Hollywood, I learned a lot about disguises. I could make us look quite different, and people would think we were college students in D.C. on vacation." Jessica's smile broadened. "I think it would work."

"Wait a minute. What's with the 'we' again?"

"Dad, no one goes on vacation alone. I'd be part of his disguise."

"No!" Brett roared.

"Jessica?" a male voice called from the bedroom.

"Oh, Dad, you woke him up." Jessica hurried to the bedroom.

"What's wrong?" Steve demanded as she came through the door.

"It's just Dad protesting about my plans. How are you feeling?"

"Fine. What plans?"

Brett stepped into the bedroom behind Jessica. "Plans that put her with you in D.C."

"What? You're not going with me to D.C., Jess! That's too dangerous!" Steve pushed himself up from his pillows.

"I'm beginning to like you better, young man." Brett stuck out his hand.

Steve fell back against his pillow with an abrupt laugh. "Great minds," he muttered. "I'm Steve Carter," he said, reaching up to shake the proffered hand.

"Brett Randall."

Jessica glared at them. "I'm glad you're both happy, but I'm not!" she exclaimed.

Brett rolled his eyes, and Steve ignored her.

"Mr. Randall, could I get you to lend me a hand

so I can get to the bathroom?" he asked, ignoring Jessica's complaint.

With a disdainful sniff, Jessica returned to the kitchen.

Brett turned to the bed to help Steve. Then he stopped dead in his tracks and frowned. "Who slept in the bed with you?"

Steve turned bright red.

"WILL STEVE BE READY to eat in five minutes?" Anna asked.

"I suppose so. He's getting Dad to assist him to the bathroom right now. They find themselves in complete agreement!"

"It doesn't sound like you're in agreement," Anna pointed out.

"No, I'm not. I won't stay home and be a good girl!" Jessica stomped over to the sofa and plopped down.

"It would be safer," Anna said.

"For me, yes, but not for Steve. He can't pretend to be a tourist on his own. No one would believe him."

"Give me the details to the plan you've concocted," Anna asked, coming over to join her daughter on the sofa.

Jessica explained her plan as it had come to her. "I can do this, Mom. I know I can."

"But you have to agree that it could be dangerous," her mother pointed out.

"If we make the right preparations, it should go okay. He'll need blue contacts, a bleach job on his hair, some jeans, boots and…a letter jacket!" Jessica exclaimed in delight as the picture became complete in her head.

"But what about getting you away from here? Wouldn't that be difficult?"

"Mike said he could handle that part of the plan."

The bedroom door opened and the two men emerged.

Anna stood. "Oh, good. Perfect timing. Lunch is ready."

"Good, because I'm starved," Steve said with a smile. Then he extended a hand. "I believe you've been here before, but I don't remember. I'm Steve Carter, and you must be Jessica's mother."

"Yes, I am. How are you feeling?"

"Much better than the last time you were here. Your daughter has been taking good care of me."

"Glad to hear that." Anna smiled at him. "Now let's eat."

Steve ate a good meal, more than he had been eating. Jessica kept a sharp eye on him, but she tried to hide that fact from her parents.

When lunch was over, she suggested they leave the dishes for later and have a visit.

The two men had already moved to the living room. When the ladies joined them, Brett said,

"Steve and I are in agreement that Jessica shouldn't go to D.C. with him."

"So?" Jessica asked, a challenge in her voice.

"So that settles it."

"It certainly does not!"

"Steve," Anna said, catching the other man's attention, "have you heard Jessica's plan?"

"I heard that she wants to go to D.C. with me. That would be too dangerous, Mrs. Randall. I can't allow that."

"I think you should hear the details of her plan before you say no," she said gently.

"Anna!" Brett protested. "Whose side are you on?"

"Sweetheart, I'm not taking sides. I just suggested that Jessica have the opportunity to explain."

Steve looked at Jessica. "Okay, explain it to me."

Jessica explained her young tourists plan in great detail. Then she sat silently while Steve gave it some thought.

"Do you really think we could pull it off?"

"Of course, Steve. You've been undercover for a long time. This is simply another role. And I've been doing it for three years. With proper preparation, no one will recognize you. And if Dad can arrange an appointment, no one will suspect a thing."

"I'll admit, Jess, it's not as wild as I thought it would be. It might even work," Steve said, frowning.

"Steve, you said you didn't think it was a good idea," Brett reminded him, alarm rising in his voice.

"But, Mr. Randall, I hadn't heard her idea," Steve explained.

"Even if her idea is a good one, you could go with someone else. It doesn't have to be Jess," Brett said.

"Yes, it does!" Jessica returned. "*I* saved him."

"Jess, your dad is right. It'll still be dangerous. Maybe someone else could—"

Anna stepped in to calm the tempers. "I think we can make that decision later. Right now Brett needs to contact whoever he knows in D.C. to get the appointment. Until that happens, there's no need to make any decisions."

"You're right, Mrs. Randall."

"Please, call me Anna. There are way too many Mrs. Randalls."

"Yes, I heard there were a lot of you," Steve added with a grin that seemed to charm Anna.

Brett moved over and sat on the arm of the sofa, putting his arm around Anna. "*My wife* is a reasonable woman. And the center of my universe," Brett said fiercely. "I'm not losing her to some smooth-talking stranger."

Steve tried to jump to his feet, but he fell back down onto the sofa. "Sir, I wasn't trying to flirt with your wife."

Jessica hurried to his side. "You've been up long enough. It's time for you to go back to bed." She helped him to his feet and led him to the bedroom.

As soon as Steve and Jessica left the room, Anna turned on her husband. "Brett Randall, shame on you. You know no one is going to steal me away from you!" She gave him a light kiss. "Now, I need to go check his wound. Do you feel the need to supervise me?

"No, but be sure he behaves himself."

AFTER HER PARENTS LEFT, Jessica returned to the bedroom where Steve lay. The late-afternoon sun slanted into the room, bathing him in light. He was awake, she could see, facing the door on his side, but he didn't acknowledge her arrival.

"Did your dad forgive me?" He spoke but he stayed still, not looking at her.

She walked farther into the room and stood beside him. "He knew you weren't flirting with my mother. But he gets jealous anyway. I hope you're not angry with him."

"No, it's kind of cute, actually." He turned onto his back and there was a hint of a smile on his face.

"Remember when you were a kid and you were so embarrassed to see your parents kissing?" Jessica asked.

The smile disappeared and he shook his head. "I don't remember that."

Those memories were so vivid for her. How could he not recall them? Did his parents not love each other, or— "Were your parents divorced?"

Steve drew a deep breath. "Yeah. Ever since I was about six months old, I'm told."

"So you didn't know your father?"

"Not at all."

"How sad for you. And for your mom. Does she still live in L.A.?"

Steve shifted under the covers, drawing his leg up as if trying to shield himself from her probing questions. "She's dead, Jess." He blew out a breath. "She was a druggie, so dependent on that poison that she didn't care what happened to me. Half the time she didn't even know I existed."

"Oh, Steve, I'm sorry," She reached for him then, her hands cupping his face as she sat beside him on the bed. "How old were you when she died?"

"Twelve. But she'd already left me several years earlier. I was in a foster home when she died."

Filled with empathy, she couldn't resist. She bent over and wrapped him in her arms.

He accepted her hug, even encouraged it, his arm going around her shoulder. When she turned her head to him and their lips were mere millimeters from each other, he didn't turn away as she covered the distance.

His lips felt soft and warm, their touch gentle and

tentative. An exploration. And invitation. The kiss was everything she thought it would be. Until he suddenly jerked back.

"We can't do this," he said in a choked voice. "I promised your father."

Jessica stared at him. "What did you promise my father?"

"He—he noticed that the second pillow was indented and he wanted to know who'd been sleeping in the bed with me." He didn't look at her as he spoke. "I couldn't lie to him!"

"Why not? You've been working undercover for a long time. What's one little lie?"

His gaze shot to hers. "Because this wasn't undercover. This was real. I told him it wasn't what it looked like. That we weren't…messing around."

"So now you're saying I'm wrong to kiss you?"

"Of course you are, Jess. I have no future, remember?"

Reining in the anger that threatened to break out, she asked, "I thought my plan sounded good to you."

Steve reached out for her. "Jess, I—"

"Shh!" she warned him, turning from him to stare into the living room. "Did you hear that?"

Steve struggled to rise, but Jessica pushed him back on the bed. "Stay here," she whispered.

Jessica padded silently into the living room, picking up her gun first. After taking off the safety, she grabbed the phone and dialed the sheriff's office, her gaze fixed on the front door.

"Sheriff's office," said a voice on the other end of the line.

"I need to talk to Mike right away," she whispered.

"I beg your pardon? I can't hear you."

"Get me Mike now," she said urgently just as someone knocked on the door.

She didn't make a move toward the door. She had a weird feeling about whoever was out there. They made no attempt to let her know who it was.

From the phone came a voice, "This is Mike."

"It's Jess," she said in a barely audible tone. There's someone—"

Then the fireworks started.

After the first shot, Jessica moved just inside the bedroom, holding the gun pointed to the floor, waiting, as Mike had said.

Since she'd dropped the phone, she figured Mike would be right up there, but she wasn't sure there would be time for him to rescue them.

"Jess?" Steve yelled. She heard him hit the floor. She hoped he stayed down there.

The door, what was left of it, slammed back against the wall and a man came through it, tall and lean but obviously strong and capable.

Jessica knew instantly this was one of Steve's

former partners, one of the guys she'd seen here before, and she opened fire. After what she thought
were four rapid-fire shots, he fell to the ground. Her
eyes shot to the door but no one else followed him in.

Mike came pounding up the stairs. "Jess!" he
yelled.

"Come in, Mike. It's clear," she called. She held
her gun so that the barrel pointed up at the ceiling,
but her hand was shaking.

Mike's appearance in the doorway relieved her
somewhat.

He bent next to the man lying on the floor in her
doorway. After feeling for a pulse, he shook his head.
Then he stepped over him and came to Jessica. He
took the gun from her limp hand. "It's okay, Jess.
You did good."

Just then Steve managed to crawl through the
door of the bedroom.

"Jess!" he called, panic in his voice. "What happened?"

He reached for Jessica and pulled her down into
his arms as he sat on the floor. She curled up against
him, burying her face in his neck.

"Jess protected you by shooting this guy," Mike
explained. "Can you identify him?"

"Yeah, in a minute," Steve said, keeping his attention focused on Jessica. "Honey, are you all
right?"

She nodded, but she didn't raise her head.

"You didn't get hit, did you?"

She shook her head.

"I need to go identify the guy. Why don't you go in the bedroom and wait for me."

Shielding her eyes from the body on the floor, Jessica hurried to the bedroom.

Mike came around to help Steve to his feet.

"Doesn't Jess's sister live nearby?" Steve asked as he stood. "I think we should call her to be with Jess."

"Actually, she's across the street. She's probably outside now." Mike moved to the door and called for Tori, motioning with his arm.

"She's coming. You got something we can cover the body with?"

Steve stepped back into the bedroom and pulled the top sheet off the bed. There was no sign of Jess, who obviously was in the bathroom.

Mike just got the body covered as Tori reached the top of the stairs.

"Mike! What happened? Where's Jessica?"

"She's fine. Just a little shook up. Steve thought maybe she'd need to talk to you."

Steve was standing by the sofa. "She's in the bathroom, I think."

Tori gingerly stepped over the shrouded white mound on the floor, without asking any more questions.

Once she'd closed the bedroom door, Mike turned a serious expression to Steve. "I've got to find out what went wrong this time. This guy was one of your partners, right?"

Steve moved over to the body and raised the sheet. "Yeah. That's Marcus."

"Okay, I'm going to send a couple of deputies up here while I go check on my man who was supposed to be watching the stairs. I'll be back as soon as I can."

Steve sank onto the sofa. The door was shot up, and several bullets were in the sofa, too. There was a pool of blood forming on the floor. He was going to owe for a lot of damages. But Jessica had saved his life once again.

He hadn't even known Jessica had a gun, much less knew how to use it so effectively. He'd only glanced at the body, but the shots had all been centered in the torso, he'd noticed. He felt bad about Marcus, but there was no way to save him, and he'd done more than enough damage with his dope dealing to merit his death.

Steve heard steps on the stairs and tensed, but it was Mike along with several other men. He carried a body bag that he handed to two of the men, his deputies. The other one, in street clothes, followed Mike into the room.

"Steve, I don't think you've met Jessica's cousin, Russ Randall. He and Jess's sister, Tori, are partners in the accounting firm across the street."

"Hello," Steve said, offering his hand.

"Glad to meet you."

"I don't think Jess's dad was glad to meet me," Steve returned. "Especially after the trouble I've gotten his daughter in."

Mike was giving orders to his men. "Don't zip up the bag or move him yet. Jon's coming to pronounce him dead." Then he turned back to Steve. "We're going to have to move you out of here until we get some repairs done."

"Yeah. I'm sorry about that. I'll be glad to pay for them."

"Don't worry about it. I'm sure the family will chip in the money."

"But—"

Russ interrupted his protest. "Listen to Mike, Steve. We Randalls have the money. Tori invests the money for all of us, and she's a near genius about the stock market."

So, Steve remarked to himself, it seemed the Randall women were as smart as they were beautiful.

But were they safe? Especially one Jessica Randall?

Because as Steve heard footsteps thundering up the stairs, he suddenly realized that though Marcus was no longer a threat, his partner was still out there.

Chapter Eight

Mike moved to the door to intercept the new arrival.

He breathed a sigh of relief when he saw Brett. Immediately, he said, "She's fine, Brett, I promise."

"What happened? It looks like World War III took place here!" Brett exclaimed, his gaze focused on the body. "Is Steve okay, too?"

"Yes, he's fine." Mike gestured to Steve, talking with Russ.

"So where's Jessica?" Brett demanded.

"She's in the bedroom with her sister. Jess was a little shaken by what happened and we thought— Steve thought Tori could steady her."

Brett walked over to Steve and slapped him on the shoulder. Unfortunately, it was the shoulder that had been shot, and Steve's knees buckled.

Russ reached for him and got him to the sofa.

"Sorry, I forgot about the shoulder wound." Brett

sat next to him. "Hey, there are even holes in the sofa. How could this happen?"

"There was a second man who knocked my deputy on the head while his partner went up the stairs," Mike explained in disgust.

"So there's still one out there?" Brett asked, anxiety building in his voice. "How are you going to protect Jess now?"

Mike rubbed the back of his neck. "I was kind of thinking she and Steve should go to the ranch. Would you consider that? I know it would put all of you in danger, but—"

Brett didn't need time to think. He shot to his feet. "I think it's a great idea. Let's get packed up."

MOST OF THE RANDALL family showed up at the ranch that evening for a welcome-home dinner for Jessica. Steve watched in amazement as he was introduced to yet another Randall. He'd already met thirty or forty of them, he was sure.

"It's a pleasure to meet you, Nick. You're related to Jessica how?"

Nick Randall smiled. "I'm a second cousin, though I didn't discover that fact until a couple of years ago. I was adopted shortly after I was born. You've probably met my twin, Gabe Randall."

"That explains it. Here I thought I was seeing double." Steve nodded in amusement. "Jessica certainly has a big family."

"Isn't it amazing?" Nick asked with an understanding look. "There was only me and my parents. After they died, I felt disconnected, lost. Then I discovered my real identity and found this terrific family. And my wife." His smile softened. "I met Sarah, and my life changed. We have two children now."

"Congratulations. That's wonderful." Steve's gaze traveled to Jessica before he'd realized it.

Beside him, Nick laughed. "I can see you've fallen too, huh?"

"What?" Steve regrouped suddenly and followed Nick's line of thinking. This newest Randall thought he was smitten with Jessica. "No! Not me! I was just—I need to sit down. I've been standing too long."

"I heard you had a gunshot wound," Nick said. "Are you in pain?"

Steve sat down on the nearby sofa and before he could answer, Jessica appeared at his side.

"Are you all right, Steve?" Her concern was obvious.

"I just needed to sit down, Jess. Relax. Sit with me. You certainly have a big family," he said, looking around the living room filled with Randalls. With all the people and activity he worried that someone could slip in easily.

After the shooting, Mike and his men had circled the town but there was no sign of Baldwin. They were sure he'd run as soon as the shooting had begun.

But what would prevent him from returning?

"Uh, Jess, is Mike here?"

Nick said, "I saw him come in a few minutes ago. Want me to bring him over?"

"If you don't mind, I'd appreciate it," Steve replied.

"What do you need Mike for?" Jessica asked.

"I just don't think it's safe here. What if—"

"The dogs will alert us if any stranger comes near. Especially Murphy. He's here in the house with us."

"I know, but…I could endanger your entire family, and they're a really special group of people."

Jessica stared at him. "You didn't have a family, did you?"

"No, I didn't. I told you I was in foster care. Your family is a real gift, Jess, and I don't want anything to happen to them."

"You're not going anywhere, Steve," Jessica said. "Not until you agree to my plan."

"Your father is not going to forgive me if I let you go to D.C. with me, Jess. I'd like to be able to come back here, but that won't happen if you go with me."

"It might not happen if I don't go with you," Jessica protested, her hands on her trim hips. "My plan will keep you safe. And it will bring you back home safely."

"Jess, I don't belong here. I don't have a way to support myself here. I'm not a cowboy, or a lawyer or—"

"Or a lawman?" a deep voice asked.

Steve turned to see Mike standing there.

"Not the kind you are, Mike," he explained. "I don't think I should stay here. You know as well as I do that the other guy wouldn't hesitate to kill innocent people if it led to me."

"Yeah, I know that. And I explained it to Brett and his brothers, just to be sure. They still insisted you stay here."

"Mike, you've got to understand—"

Mike patted him on his good shoulder. "I understand, Steve. More than you can grasp. I'm leaving two deputies here to help out. They'll maintain guard during the nights. All you have to do is get stronger and think about Jess's plan. I think it might work, too."

Steve looked at all the good people in the room and shook his head. "I don't know."

"Yes, Steve, you know. It's the best way, like Mike said. You're safe here," Jessica assured him. "You just need another couple of days to be strong enough to go to D.C. With me."

"Your dad—"

"I'm not a child, Steve. And we shouldn't be having this discussion in the middle of a family reunion!" Obviously finished arguing, Jessica stood up and walked away.

Steve's gaze never left her retreating figure, until Mike whispered, "Watch out, or you're going to be part of the family sooner than you expected."

"What are you talking about?"

Mike grinned. "It didn't take me long to figure out Caro was for me, even if the family was a little overwhelming."

"No, I—I don't have a future, Mike. I have to turn these guys in, and it may cost me my life. I don't want to— I can't—" He broke off, staring at Mike.

"Things will work out, Steve. This is the safest place you can be right now. And in the future."

Steve was beginning to think the whole family was crazy. Couldn't they see the difficulty?

Steve had been trying to shut out the warmth that stole over him whenever Jessica was with him. The urge to pull her close and kiss her, caress her. He couldn't make her promises. He couldn't offer her a future.

Like a moth, his gaze traveled helplessly around the room to the vibrant flame that Jessica was. It was easy to believe she'd been a success in Hollywood. She would light up a screen.

What was he doing even thinking about Jessica? He had to get out of here. "Mike, I need to ask you something."

Mike sat down beside him. "What is it?"

"I don't have my gun. How can I get a new one?"

"I don't know. Why do you need one? You can't take it on the flight to D.C., and the Randalls have plenty of guns to protect you. I don't think you need one."

"But—"

Mike patted him on his good shoulder again and left him sitting there.

Now what? Maybe he could borrow Jessica's gun.

That certainly wasn't what he wanted from her. But under the circumstances, it would have to do.

JESSICA WAS SURROUNDED by her family all evening, but she always knew where Steve was. She tried to hide her observation of him, but her sister, Tori, knew.

"If you don't look away from him, everyone's going to realize how interested you are."

"But I'm responsible for him, Tori. I brought him into the family. And I have to keep all of them safe."

"That's the only reason you can't take your eyes off him?" Tori teased. "I think you're overdoing the safety thing."

"I don't think so."

"Mom's already noticed," Tori warned.

Jessica's gaze flew to her mother, standing across the room. Her mother looked up at that moment and smiled at her. Jessica turned back to her sister. "I don't think she's noticed. She hasn't said anything."

"Mom wouldn't. She understands how it strikes you. That's what happened between her and Dad. And he was engaged to someone else."

"I didn't know that."

Tori smiled. "She doesn't spread that around. But what they felt for each other kind of broke up the engagement."

"I saved him, Tori. I have to take care of him."

"What happens when he's well? When he doesn't need you to save him?"

"He's never had a family. There was only him and his mom, and she—she got hooked on drugs. He was put in foster care two years before she died. So you see, I can save him even when he's safe. I can save him with family."

"Be careful, sister. It has to be about the two of you, not the family, if you want it to last."

"I know," Jessica said with a sigh. "But I'm not sure—" She paused before adding, "I'll be careful."

She joined her parents as people began to leave, saying goodbye and thanking them for coming. She knew Steve was still sitting on the sofa, talking to Red and Mildred. They'd been so busy preparing food for the gathering, they hadn't actually talked with Steve until now.

When finally only the residents of the ranch were left, which was still a fair number of people, Mildred suggested Jessica take Steve to his room for the night.

Jessica immediately summoned Murphy to escort them. "Are the deputies on duty?" she asked as she moved to Steve's side.

"Yes, they are," Brett said. "We're taking your protection seriously, honey. You and Steve are safe."

Jessica stretched up to kiss him on the cheek. "Thanks, Dad."

"Yeah, I appreciate your assistance," Steve said, stretching out a hand for Brett to shake.

"No problem. We've let the dogs out tonight, too, to make sure no one slips through."

"Thank you," Steve said quietly.

"And, Dad, tomorrow you'll make the call to your contact in D.C.?" Jessica asked. "Like we talked about earlier?"

"I'll see what I can do, but I'm not sure I have the right connections," Brett said, looking doubtful.

"I'm sure you do, Dad." Jessica gave him another kiss before she turned to Steve. "Do you need help getting up?"

"No, I can get up," Steve said, showing he could by standing. "You can just tell me where my bedroom is and I'll find it by myself," he added.

"The house is too big and complicated, Steve. It'll be easier for me to show you," Jessica assured him as she took his arm. She loved the feel of him. Her cheeks heated up as she remembered her sister's warning.

"Good night," she called out to the family as she

led Steve to the stairs. "All your things were taken up earlier," she told him as they climbed the flight.

"What things? I don't have anything."

"You have the clothes we've loaned you. I washed them this afternoon, and some of the family contributed more things so you'd feel more comfortable."

Steve shook his head. "But, Jessica, I don't want to owe anyone else. I already owe you my life!"

"You wish I'd left you dying in that alley?" she demanded, irritation on her face.

"Of course I don't, but— Jess, I can't—"

"You can't what?"

"There are no guarantees in my lifestyle. You know that. All I have is this moment. And I'm not even sure of that."

"We're safe here."

"I'm not so sure. I wish I had a gun. Will you loan me yours?"

"I'm not sure that would be wise. I'll have to check with your doctor."

"But that leaves me with nothing to protect myself."

Jessica opened a door. "Here's your bedroom. We'll talk in the morning."

"Wait, Jessica—"

But Jessica ignored him and left the bedroom.

When she reached her room, she sat down in front

of the dresser mirror. "What should I do?" she asked Murphy, who'd followed at her heels. The dog whined and laid his head on her knees.

Jessica petted him. "I don't know, Murphy. I know I don't own him, but I don't want him to leave. Not without me. And if I give him my gun, I'm afraid he'll try to slip away so he won't involve me or my family. I can't let him do that."

She stood and began pacing the room. "But I can't leave him unprotected, either. Like him, I'm not sure."

She decided to make her choice after she'd had a shower.

When she was done, she dressed in a long silk nightgown she'd bought in California. Then she combed her red curls and creamed her flawless skin. Murphy whined again, and she knelt to hug him. "I'm going to talk things over with Steve. I want you to stay here, but let me know if you hear anything strange."

The last thing she did was take her gun from the suitcase. She carefully loaded it again and put on the safety. She wasn't going to give it to Steve, but she would use it to protect him if she needed to.

Slipping into a matching robe and placing the gun in the robe's pocket, she checked her hair one more time, petted Murphy and slipped out of her bedroom, tiptoeing down the hall.

Her bedroom wasn't far from Steve's, a fact for which she was grateful. Otherwise, she might run into the parents as they came up to bed. With four sets of them, she'd be in trouble no matter which way she went. Growing up, the Randall kids had learned all four sets of parents could dole out punishment and didn't keep secrets from one another.

A smile flitted across her face as she remembered a few times that she'd been caught. But that wasn't going to happen tonight.

When she reached the door to Steve's room, she thought about knocking, but decided against it. Instead, she opened the door and slipped inside.

Strong arms grabbed her and threw her against the wall.

"Wait!" she shrieked.

Steve stared at her. "Jessica! What are you doing here?" he asked in a harsh tone.

"I—I came to protect you," she said in return.

"Damn it, Jess, you can't keep saving me! I'll never be able to repay you." Steve stepped back.

"Is your shoulder all right?" Jessica asked, her gaze staring at his right shoulder.

"It's still a little weak, but I can defend myself," he assured her.

Jessica took a step toward him. "But I don't think it's safe for you to be alone."

Chapter Nine

"Jess, I promised your father!" Steve protested even as his arms went around her.

"I didn't," she said succinctly, raising her lips toward his.

He wasn't a robot. Or a dead man. When a beautiful redhead wanted a kiss, he was willing to comply. At least he had been in the past. But he wasn't playacting now, as he had so many times, and that made his reaction even more important.

"Jess, I only have now, this moment. I can't promise—"

"I didn't ask for promises, Steve. No one can promise a future, because the future is unknown. I want now."

He bent his head and their lips met. He'd kissed women, all kinds of women, but this one was different. Her kiss was giving, warm, intense. He pulled her tighter against him, wanting more....

But the sound of gunshots broke them apart.

Jessica pushed him back and pulled out her revolver. Cautiously she looked out the window but saw nothing amiss. She was about to check the house when the bedroom door opened.

Her father stuck his head in.

"Dad, what's happening?"

"Apparently, a man challenged one of the deputies. He got away, but the deputy took a bullet in his leg. I called Mike. He's on his way. Your mom went to tend to the deputy."

"He'll probably come back tonight, thinking he can avoid the deputies now that he knows they're on duty," Steve said, frowning.

"Why would he do that?" Brett asked. "He's facing injury or death."

"He'd come back because his life is at stake. If I make it to D.C. and turn in the proof of what they've been doing, he'll spend the rest of his life in prison. Lawmen don't fare well in prison, so he might as well be dead." Steve said the last part with anger in his tone. "Damn, I knew this would happen. I knew I'd bring danger to this ranch."

Jessica put a finger to his lips, but Steve wouldn't be stopped.

He stepped around her. "Please, sir," he said to Brett, "she thinks she needs to protect me, but I'm trying to convince her I can manage on my own if she'll just lend me her gun."

"That's not possible," Brett said. "You haven't recovered enough. That would be suicide."

"Mr. Randall, you don't want Jess in the middle of things, and neither do I. If I had a gun, I could get out of here and remove the danger. I can guarantee he'll follow me."

Jessica sent Steve a disgusted look. "Of course he will, unless he's an idiot! But you wouldn't be safer, one on one, than you are here, surrounded by people who care about you!"

"But I never—"

Steve broke off as they all heard a vehicle coming down the driveway.

"That will be Mike," Brett said. "I'm going downstairs." He looked at the two of them, his glance lingering on Jessica's nightgown and Steve's bare chest. "Anyone coming down should get dressed."

Jessica tensed, but instead of arguing, she marched out of Steve's room to her own.

ALONE WITH BRETT, Steve went on the offensive. "I need some jeans and boots so I can get out of here before Jessica realizes it."

But Brett gave him no quarter. "Much as I don't want my daughter mixed up in this, I have to agree with her that sending you out on your own would be crazy. Let's go talk to Mike."

Downstairs, the men of the family were gathered in the kitchen. Someone had made a pot of coffee, and it seemed everyone had a cup in his hand.

When he noticed the sheriff, Steve asked, "How's the deputy?"

"He's taken a bullet in the leg. We're going to get him to the hospital, but he'll be all right. I've got another man to replace him."

"I've got to get out of here," Steve protested in a low voice. "I'm endangering this family, and they don't deserve that!"

Mike looked Steve in the eye. "You want me to take a vote? Whether to send you out on your own or to keep you here, protected?" With a smile, he added, "I know the way the vote will go. The Randalls aren't weak or selfish."

Jessica entered the room, determination on her face. "Where is Steve?" she demanded.

He stepped out from behind Mike. "I'm here, Jess, but—"

"No buts about it. You have to give my plan a chance to work! I insist on it!"

"She's got a point, Steve." Mike grinned when Jessica sent him a triumphant look. "Let's wait until tomorrow and see what Brett can do with his phone calls. Then we can make a decision."

"By then, someone else could be injured or killed protecting me! I don't want that!"

Jake put a hand on his shoulder. "We know you didn't ask to come here and let us protect you. We made that decision, and we'll deal with the danger that it may bring. You haven't even healed yet."

"I'm almost well. I heal fast. If I had a gun and some jeans and boots, I'd be all right." He looked around, searching for anyone who'd help him out.

No one volunteered.

Then Mike spoke up. "My deputy said he got a shot off and thought he might've winged the guy, so I don't expect him back tonight. Just give us the night, Steve, and we'll work things out tomorrow."

"I guess I don't have much choice," Steve growled.

"No, you don't!" Jessica agreed, a grim smile on her face. "You have to give my plan a chance to work."

"Honey, these men aren't going to be confused because I put on a hat or wear glasses. They *know* me. We've worked together for years."

"I can fool them. I know it. It's not just the disguise, it's the attitude."

Steve groaned and looked around for someone to carry on the argument. Instead, he came face-to-face with Anna, Jessica's mother.

She patted him on his good shoulder. "Don't

worry about it now. Just go upstairs and get a good night's sleep."

Everyone nodded in agreement and Steve turned toward the stairs. He was surrounded by goodness. He only hoped no one got hurt until he could get out of there.

"YOUNG LADY, YOU NEED to go to bed, too. Your own bed!" Brett emphasized.

Jessica leaned up and kissed his cheek. "Good night, Dad."

Brett stared as she calmly climbed the stairs.

Anna slipped her arm through her husband's. "Your daughter will do what's right. Just like you did. Trust her."

"She's too giving."

"Just like her daddy," Anna said again. "Come on, we need to get our rest, too. I'm feeling my age tonight."

"Not you, Anna. You still look as young as Jessica," Brett whispered, his arm going around his wife's waist.

"When you hold me, I feel as young as Jessica," she told him with a warm smile, moving him up the stairs to their room.

STEVE LAY AWAKE for a while, afraid his enemy would come back and harm someone else. He was desperately frustrated. The situation was ridiculous! He should get up and steal a gun and clothes from these good people, and stop them from sacrificing themselves.

But he couldn't bring himself to do such a rotten thing to them. Jess, for one, would never forgive him. He didn't want to disappoint her.

He began to relax, his body taking advantage of the safe warm bed....

Until he felt greater warmth as another body wrapped around his.

His arms surrounded Jessica, pulling her close in spite of himself. Since he'd been shot, Jessica had been beside him every step of the way. He'd missed her tonight. But here she was.

When she was in his arms, all was right with his world.

JESSICA KNEW her parents, her father in particular, wouldn't approve of her behavior. But she needed to stay close to Steve. She told herself it was because she could protect him.

But when she touched him, she knew that was a lie. She didn't want to protect him. She wanted to love him.

When she awoke the next morning, she lay in the bed, pressed against Steve's side, trying to force herself to get up and let him continue to sleep. When he moved and suddenly blinked his eyes, that choice was gone.

She raised up and kissed him. Immediately he turned to her, holding her close. Together they raised the room temperature what felt like fifteen degrees. With their eyes they examined each other's body, till finally Jessica reached out a hand and traced the muscles he had developed over the years.

Steve was fascinated with her curves, her fragility. Yet he knew she was a smart, capable woman. He couldn't believe she wanted him. Never one to turn down his dream, he kissed her senseless. Almost of its own accord, their clothing disappeared until they were both naked under the sheets.

Steve told himself he shouldn't do what he was doing. But Jessica encouraged him. She was so sweet and yet so strong. A rare combination in a woman.

Unable to resist what his body wanted, Steve made love to Jessica, tasting her, memorizing her beautiful body in case he never had this opportunity again. That thought intensified his lovemaking, because he wanted her again…and again.

He tried not to look at the future. He never had. But a future without Jessica wouldn't be worth living. Though he didn't tell her he loved her, he realized he did.

When she presented him with a condom, whispering that she didn't want to get pregnant until everything was settled down, he was a goner. The thought of the two of them making a baby, having a future, was overwhelming.

Almost as overwhelming as the finale of their lovemaking. After they climaxed simultaneously Steve held her close as he regained his breath. When he attempted to speak, Jessica pressed her fingers over his lips.

"No, you don't have to promise anything, Steve. Just don't shut me out. I can help you, I promise."

"I could never shut you out, Jess, but I want to keep you safe. You're a rare woman. A special woman. I want—"

"Me, too. Let's trust that there will be a future…for us." With a sweet smile, she slipped from the bed and put on her robe, gathering up the nightgown and panties she'd worn.

"After your shower, come downstairs for some breakfast," she said as she left his bedroom.

Steve lay there, remembering, memorizing, the wonderful sensations of making love to Jessica. He didn't ever want to forget what he'd experienced as the sun rose that morning.

JESSICA LOOKED UP AS Steve entered the kitchen. She'd begun to wonder if she should go check on him. He'd taken an awfully long time to come down.

"Morning, Steve. How are you today?" she asked, as if she hadn't spent the night with him.

"Fine. Sorry if I overslept." He nodded to Red and Mildred, who were also in the kitchen.

"You've been hurt, boy," Red reminded him. "You need your rest."

"And some good food," Mildred suggested. "I made cinnamon rolls this morning. I'll warm one up for you."

As she did, she poured him a cup of coffee.

"Thank you, Mildred," Steve said, then addressed Red. "Were there any other disturbances during the night? Any word on the attacker? And what about the deputy who was wounded?"

Red looked at Jessica. "He's full of questions, isn't he?"

"Yes," Jessica agreed. "He likes to know what's going on." She, not Red, answered Steve. "I talked to Dad this morning. The deputy is fine, in the hospital recovering. There's been no sign of the attacker, but there are still a couple of deputies guarding us. And yes, they got cinnamon rolls, too."

Her words were perfectly timed as Mildred put Steve's plate in front of him. When he tasted the cinnamon roll, the rich sweetness filled him. "Wow, this is great, Mildred. You and Red are terrific cooks." Then, after a quick glance at Jessica, he said, "Does Jess know how to make these? If she does, I might have to marry her!" He laughed, hoping they would think he was joking.

In actual fact, he'd marry Jessica whether she

could cook or not…if he could. But until he believed he had a future, he couldn't.

Jessica ignored his joke. "Dad made some calls and set up a meeting for us with the head of the DEA."

Steve looked up at Jessica. "When?" he demanded.

"In three days, which gives us two days to perfect our camouflage and then board a plane to D.C."

"But, Jess, they'll be looking for me at the airlines. I can't—"

"We won't use your identity, Steve," Jessica told him patiently. "Or mine. We're going to borrow some IDs so we can get on the plane without them realizing it."

"Borrow some IDs? What are you talking about?"

"Eat your cinnamon roll. Red is scrambling eggs for you, and you don't want them to get cold. I'll explain everything after breakfast," Jessica assured him.

He wanted to shout, to insist, to tell her his life was hanging in the balance. But he not only had to be strong enough for the trip in three days, he had to be prepared. He'd learned to take life step by step. The first step was breakfast.

To that end he dug in to the plate of sausage, scrambled eggs and toast that Mildred brought him.

Jessica watched him eat with gusto. No doubt she'd encouraged him with that tidbit of news from her father. She was encouraged, too. It meant her family was finally taking her plan seriously.

The Randall clan had always been supportive of whatever the children wanted to do, but three years ago there had been a lot of doubts about her ability to crack Hollywood's horde of would-be actresses. She had stayed long enough to prove that she could act.

She'd decided she preferred life in Rawhide to life in Hollywood. With her film coming out in spring, she could return home, a proved success. But even more so, if she could pull off her plan with Steve, she would prove herself to her family once and for all.

When Steve had finished his breakfast, she suggested they stroll down to the barn and back to strengthen his muscles.

"Will it be safe?"

"Of course it will. No one can be that close, or they'd be seen. Besides, you have to get some exercise before you can go to D.C."

"You're right about that," he agreed.

Red had overheard her suggestion, and his only comment was to let the deputy know.

"We will, Red," Steve said. "And thank both of you for that fabulous breakfast. Best I've ever had," he assured them with a smile.

Outside, they took Red's advice.

"It should be safe," Harry, one of Mike's deputies, said. "But when you're out in the open, move quickly. You don't want to give anyone a stationary target."

Jessica assured him they would. "We shouldn't be long. We just need to build up Steve's endurance." She took Steve's hand and hurried toward the first barn.

Once they'd stepped inside the barn, she breathed a sigh of relief. "Did we move too fast for you?" she asked as Steve bent over to catch his breath.

"No, I'm fine. I—I just need to get some air."

"Good," she said, waiting for him to straighten. When he did so, she slid her arms around his neck. "Now I can tell you good morning the way I wanted," she said with a smile just before she kissed him.

Steve didn't protest. In fact, he was more than enthusiastic. The sweetness he'd tasted earlier in the morning was there. Like a miracle, she opened up to him again. He couldn't believe he was with her, alone, breathing the same air.

When they finally broke apart, Steve said, "Jess, I have to tell you—"

"No promises, remember?" Jessica said with a smile.

"You mean you don't want a future with me?"

Jessica stared at him. "Of course I do, but I understand that you can't promise anything. Your job is dangerous…and in California." She ducked her head and then looked at him. "I can't leave Rawhide again. I don't like living there. I know we can't plan a future, but we can share now."

He didn't argue with her. He couldn't. But he didn't object to a little more consolation. He pulled her back into his arms.

When they emerged from the barn, their arms were interlocked around each other and their gazes didn't go any farther than the other's face. They were in a fog, unaware of their surroundings.

The crack of gunfire brought them back to reality quickly. A bullet hit the ground at Steve's foot.

With well-trained reflexes, he pulled Jessica with him and rolled their bodies behind one of the trucks parked nearby.

"What was it?" Jessica asked, panting.

"Probably has a long-range rifle with a scope. I should've thought of that. I can't believe I let you distract me!"

"Well, excuse me! I didn't mean to cause problems for you!" She jumped to her feet and ran to the house.

Steve, stunned by her action, rose to follow her, but Harry shouted for him to stay down.

Damn. He'd let his attention wander to Jess again! Now it was time to come back to reality…and try to survive until tomorrow.

Chapter Ten

Damn! He'd missed again. Steve seemed to be having a run of good luck. When he'd followed Steve's entourage home last night, he'd thought he could manage a break-in to destroy Steve. But he hadn't realized how big the house would be.

Then, he'd been surprised the sheriff would put guards on the doors. What was Steve to this family?

He'd still resolved to slip in after all their guests had disappeared, figuring the guards would fall asleep before too long.

But he'd been wrong.

He'd managed to wound the guard in front, but he'd barely gotten away before half a dozen men came out of the house. He'd had no idea that many men were inside.

But he had no choice. No matter what it took, Steve had to die.

Baldwin knew he owed his partner some retribution. After all, not all the shots fired yesterday had been Marcus's. Baldwin was sure his partner had died when he'd seen them carrying a body bag down the stairs.

He'd hung around a while longer, hiding safely, waiting to see if they brought down another body bag, in case Steve had been killed, too. But there had only been one.

So, he'd promised himself he'd make an effort for Marcus's death. If not for his partner, then because he knew he couldn't tell Miguel he'd failed.

After his attempt last night, Baldwin had given up on the possibility of breaking into the house. He'd gotten out his rifle with the scope and found a tree in the pasture that gave him a visual on the back door.

He'd sat in the tree for five hours before he'd even gotten a hint of Steve emerging. And then, damn it, his shot fell short.

But he'd been patient. They would have to return sometime. And he was determined to be ready.

WHEN STEVE FINALLY got back to the house, coming in the front door, which no one ever used, Jessica wasn't in sight. He wandered into the kitchen where Red and Mildred were. "Uh, did Jessica come through here?"

"She tore through here like a whirlwind," Red said. "Didn't even say hello."

"We got shot at," Steve said, hoping to explain Jessica's behavior.

"Don't mean she couldn't say howdy," Red returned.

Mildred slapped him on his arm. "Just like a man, expecting her to say howdy when she's all afraid."

"Where's Harry? I don't see him on the back porch," Steve asked anxiously.

"He took cover by the Bachelor Pad."

"The what?" Steve asked.

Mildred patted him on the shoulder and explained. "At one time there were so many Randalls living here—and they mostly had boys—that they decided to build sort of a house just for the men. They each have a small room, but they take their meals here."

"It's that big building out the back door," Red said.

"Yeah, I saw it." He went to the back door and called softly to Harry. "Anything going on out there, Harry? Have you spotted him?"

"I thought so. I saw a dark mass, but when I shot at it, it ran away, so I'm thinking it was probably a cow. Good thing I missed it or Jake Randall would be pretty mad at me."

"Okay, don't take any chances." Steve's biggest fear at this point was that one of the Randalls or the deputies would be killed.

That was his biggest fear until he tried to leave. Then, if Jessica was with him, he'd fear something happening to her.

When that thought struck him, he stopped. Of course, there was the reason that would convince Jess not to go with him. She would endanger him by her presence.

"I gotta find Jess," he said suddenly.

"Try upstairs," Red said, concentrating on mixing something in a big bowl.

Steve hurried away before Red realized he'd suggested Steve go to Jessica's bedroom. He was pretty sure that wasn't acceptable behavior in the Randall family.

He moved up the stairs as fast as he could. He still had to catch his breath when he reached the second floor.

He knew Jessica had said her bedroom was close to his, so he knocked on the first door and softly called her name. No response. He moved down the hall, trying each door. He even resorted to trying the doorknobs, but there was no one in any of the rooms.

Finally, he stood in the middle of the hall and shouted "Jessica!" as loud as he could, frustration overtaking him.

"Yes?" came this cool, calm voice some distance away.

"Where are you?" he shouted.

"In the office on the first floor."

No more direction than that. Didn't she realize how big this house was? He'd been in hotels a lot smaller.

Going back down the stairs was much easier, but he'd reached the limit to his stamina. He sagged against the wall, wondering if he had the strength to find her.

"Steve," someone whispered.

Steve's head jerked up and he saw Red standing in the hallway pointing to a closed door.

Steve gave him a grateful nod before he staggered to the closed door and shoved it open. Okay, so he should've knocked, but he couldn't take much more.

The sight of Jessica, calmly sitting behind a massive desk writing something, irritated the heck out of him.

He collapsed in a chair and gasped, "Next time could you leave a trail of bread crumbs?"

She gave him an innocent look. "Why would I think you would want to find me?"

"Come on, Jess. You know I didn't mean— It was because I forgot to be careful. I didn't want you to be hurt."

Apparently that wasn't sufficient groveling. She continued to write, offering no response.

"Jess, when I'm with you, I forget the danger

and—and I put us both in danger because of that. And that's why you can't go with me!"

Okay, there it was, the clincher, the grand finale. He waited for his brilliant logic to hit her.

Nothing. It was a dud.

"Jess, don't you understand?"

"Of course I understand. I have a superior brain, whether you think so or not. However, your deduction isn't sound. You see, I won't let you forget once we leave here. The only problem was that *here* has been a safe place for me all my life. Therefore, it was hard for me to expect danger. Once I leave here, I won't expect safety. Ergo, we'll both be more careful then. Do *you* understand?"

"No, Jess, it's too dangerous. You have to stay here. I promise I'll return when—if—"

As he floundered between those two words, she responded. "No, you're the one who won't understand. The day of leaving the little woman at home to knit and tend the fire is over. The little woman can do other things, like shoot a gun and make plans for our escape."

Then, as if she'd convinced him, she bent her head and continued to write.

"Damn it, Jess, what is so important that you have to write it down in the middle of a fight?" he demanded.

"Our plans, of course." She paused and when she looked at him kindly, he braced himself.

"If you can present more logical plans, plans that will guarantee your safety—" she paused, letting him know she doubted that he could do that "—then I'll be glad to listen to them."

When he opened his mouth, she raised a finger and said, "But if your plan consists of you borrowing my gun and sneaking out of here, drawing the evil man away from us and leaving us safe and sound, with you, by the way, getting screwed, you can forget it!"

"Do you ever pause to breathe?" he asked.

"No." And she returned to the paper she was writing on.

"Okay, what do you have on paper?"

"I'm not ready to show it yet. I'll let you know when I am." Her voice was as cool as when he'd first found the office.

He tried again. "But—"

"Go upstairs and get some rest. Or if you can't climb the stairs again, go to the TV room and stretch out on the sofa. I'll wake you for lunch."

"Never mind!" he exclaimed. "I don't need any lunch!" He rose and turned to go, determined not to rely on her for anything.

Jessica jumped up from behind the desk and reached him before he made it to the door. She threw her arms around him and said, "Please don't go yet, Steve. I'm sorry. You upset me so much, I lost my temper."

He wasn't sure what to think. He'd been the one yelling. "But you were so quiet, so calm."

"I know it's strange, since I have red hair, but I vent my temper in words. And I insulted you. I know you're strong, and the one with expertise and incredible courage. But I really believe I can help you. And I'm part of the plan. I wouldn't even try if I didn't think it would work. I'm no masochist!"

"Okay, honey, I believe you," he whispered, wrapping his arms around her and holding her close.

"So you'll agree?"

"Whoa there! Not yet, but I'll look at your plan when you have it ready, and try to consider it honestly."

"Okay, for that promise, I'll show you the TV room and even put a movie on for you. Then, when you get up for lunch, you'll be much stronger and able to think clearly." She gave him a brief kiss and led him to a room with several comfortable couches and lots of throw pillows.

Then she put a movie in the DVD player, enticed him to the couch and tucked a pillow under his head. He got another kiss before she slipped out of the room.

Steve lay there a moment trying to remember where he'd gone wrong. Somehow, she'd convinced him to do what he'd sworn he wouldn't do and made him feel good about it.

She was one slick customer.

JESSICA DIDN'T REVEAL her plan until after dinner that evening. Once everyone had finished eating, she asked them if they'd listen to her idea and perhaps even contribute to it.

She was hoping that they wouldn't laugh and think of it as the playacting she'd done as a child. The reason she'd gone to Hollywood was to prove that her imagination could serve some purpose.

"I think Steve and I should play the roles of tourists," she told them. "We'll be in disguise and hopefully go unnoticed. We can go into the building and make it to our appointment with the DEA head. Once we're in, Steve can show him his proof. After that we'll be safe."

"You make it sound easy," Steve said. "I'm afraid that's not the reality. They will have pronounced me a rogue agent, a bad guy. I'll bet there'll be people at the airport looking for me. Once I show my ID, I'm dead."

"You still don't understand that you won't be using your ID."

"But I can't board an aircraft as a plain citizen without ID," Steve protested.

"Of course not. You'll have ID. I'm hoping you'll be Howard Hensen."

There was a murmur around the table. Steve just looked disappointed. "Couldn't I have a better name than Howard?"

"He's a real person, Steve," Brett said, looking at

his daughter in approval. "Do you think he'll let you borrow it?"

"Probably not if *I* asked him. I thought I'd ask Mike to talk to him. And maybe promise not to give him a ticket for not having ID if they stop him for a couple of days."

B.J., Jake's wife, said, "That's such a good idea, Jess, and so much simpler than having IDs faked. Howard kind of looks like you, Steve. Not quite as handsome or as big, but close enough to pass."

"Who are you going to be, dear?" Anna asked.

"Betty Jean," Jessica returned with a big grin.

"But you're a redhead," her father pointed out. "Betty Jean has been every shade of blond that exists."

"I will have blond hair too after Betty Jean finishes with me," Jessica said.

To Steve, she added, "Betty Jean went to school with me and runs the local beauty shop in Rawhide. It's only been in existence for two years, but she's doing a good job."

"You can't go to the beauty shop to get your hair dyed." Steve was adamant, obviously not willing to negotiate. "You could be followed and kidnapped as a means to force me out."

Jake concurred. "He's got a point."

Jessica defended her plan. "That's why we won't be going to the shop. Betty Jean can come here and do both our hair."

"Both? You mean me?" Steve asked in consternation.

"Yes, you. But you're not going to be all blond. You're going to have blond tips and spike your hair."

"Oh, that's clever," Megan said. "It will immediately make people think he's younger than he is."

"Exactly, Aunt Megan. And he's going to wear jeans, boots and a leather coat lined in sheepskin. Or at least he will if someone else will go shopping in Sarah and Jen's store for me."

"You think that will be enough of a disguise, a change of shirt and a pair of boots?" Steve didn't sound remotely convinced. "I won't make it out of the airport."

"Yes, you will, if you'll listen," Jessica insisted. "We're also, assuming someone will go to Buffalo, going to change your brown eyes to blue."

"I don't think—"

"Do you have to be so resistant? I'm trying to help you. The colored contacts won't affect your vision, but they *will* change your appearance."

"Are you going to wear some?"

"No, they haven't been close enough to me to know my eye color. Besides, I have more to my disguise. I'm along to lend credence to you and to distract."

"What do you mean?" Pete asked. "I've followed everything so far, but…"

Jessica smiled at her uncle. "If they scrutinized

Steve close enough, he wouldn't fool them. But if Steve were accompanied by someone…seductive, they'd barely give him a once-over."

Her father and Steve objected vehemently and bonded again when Steve asked, "What do you mean seductive?"

"You know, general things, like I'll dress in a short skirt, low top, things like that." She wasn't willing to reveal her total disguise, especially not in front of her father. But she'd learned to play roles that had nothing to do with her, and that was exactly what she was going for.

Steve began to object again. "I don't think—"

"Couldn't you have just a *little* faith in my abilities?" Jessica demanded, hoping that would make her father reverse his opinion. Steve might not be as easily manipulated, but she figured she'd give it a go.

"Of course you have abilities, Jess," Brett said, as she'd predicted.

Steve wasn't that easy.

"This is life or death, Jess, for both of us. Guessing won't work," he growled.

"I know that. I got you here, didn't I, when you couldn't help yourself? I've helped protect you while you healed. I'm asking for one more time. If you're not convinced Friday morning, we won't board that plane."

"What else can we do?" Janie asked.

"I'll need these items bought by someone in Buffalo, too," Jessica said, sliding a piece of paper toward her mother.

"We'll also need someone to take us to the airport in Denver, preferably. I'm not too eager to change planes once we get started."

"I can do that," her father immediately offered.

Jake added, "I can ride shotgun."

"I appreciate that," Jessica told them, "but I'm afraid they might have the license plates of the ranch vehicles, which would make it easy to spot us at the airport. I was wondering if we could get Mike or Jon to drive us, once we get to Rawhide, since their last names are not Randall."

She'd known her father in particular wouldn't like that idea. There was a silence for several minutes. Then Jake said, "Much as I hate to say it, she's probably right. But maybe we could just convince one of them to swap cars with us. I bet Jon would do that. He and Tori sometimes ride together. He wouldn't even miss it."

"Good idea," Brett agreed, relieved to be a part of the plan. "I'll go call him."

After her dad left the table, Jessica said, "Thanks, Uncle Jake. That way Dad can help."

"Yeah, me too. I want to be a part of your big production," he replied with a grin.

She couldn't hold back a giggle. As a child, she'd dragged the other children into her productions and the parents had dutifully sat and watched for what had to have added up to a hundred miserable hours.

"You were all so patient when I was a child," she said with a grateful smile.

"I think it was good for all the kids," Megan said. "There wasn't anything in school that let them try different things."

Jessica stared at Megan. "I think you've given me an idea, Aunt Megan. I've been wondering what I would do now that I've come back home. I could start an acting club at the school. I could even have a little theater group here in town where adults could participate, too. What fun! I hadn't thought of that before."

Anna beamed at her daughter. "I'm just glad to hear you're planning on staying."

"Yes, Mom, I'm going to stay. I've missed life here too much to go away again." As she spoke, she looked down at her lists, avoiding Steve's gaze. But she could feel his eyes on her, burning her. An awkward moment passed.

Into that pool of silence, Chad said, "Is there anything else to do, Jess?"

"I haven't thought of anything else. That's why I wanted to tell you the plan and let you add details if they're necessary."

"Are you sure you'll be able to distract them?" Steve asked.

"I will for sure if they're men," she said, giving him a sweet smile. "But even if they're women, they won't be able to ignore me."

"Don't we want them to ignore us?"

"No, we want them to ignore *you,* not me," Jessica explained. "I'm part of your disguise. I'm going to borrow Casey's senior ring, or anyone else who can find his. And a big letter jacket. That's going to be my coat."

"You are so good at this, Jessica," her Aunt Megan said. "You get the concept and carry it out perfectly!"

"Thank you. I know it's not an essential skill, but it's the skill I have."

"But it is essential," her aunt said. "I think children need to experiment before they find their places in life. You would let them experiment with safe things, things that help them understand themselves, instead of experimenting with drugs."

"Do you have a lot of that here?" Steve asked.

"Not a lot, but it's growing here just as it is all over," Brett said as he reentered the room at the tail end of Megan's comment. "We're trying to head it off at the pass."

Steve nodded but didn't say anything.

Jessica drew a deep breath and looked at him. "So that's my plan, Steve. What do you think?"

It took him a minute, during which Jessica's heart beat ten times as fast as normal. Then he lifted his head and said, "You've got a good plan, Jess. You've convinced me."

Jessica broke into a big smile. She wanted to go around the table and hug him, but she had to be more discreet in front of her father. She settled for a courteous "Thank you, Steve."

"No, thank you, Jess, and I'm sorry I doubted you. I didn't realize how thorough you'd be. You've planned down to the smallest details in our disguises."

"Yes. Fortunately, you don't wear any jewelry and if you have any tattoos," she said, pretending she hadn't seen him naked, "we'll be able to cover them."

"Uh, yeah. I mean, no, I don't have any tattoos."

"Good. Then I think we've planned for everything."

"So you're not staying over in D.C.?" her father asked, relief in his voice.

"I don't think we'll need to. At least I won't need to. Steve may have some business that requires he be there longer, but by then he'll be out of danger."

"And you're coming home?" he asked again.

"Yes, Dad, as I said earlier, I'm here to stay."

"There may not be a lot of excitement here," Brett warned.

Janie laughed. "There will be with Jessica back in the fold. I can't imagine life being dull with her around!"

Chapter Eleven

When everyone dispersed to go to bed, Steve kept his eye on Jessica. He wanted her to come to him again tonight. It might be his last time to hold her.

When she started up the stairs, he immediately moved behind her. As soon as they were alone, he called her name softly.

She looked over her shoulder and then continued up the stairs. "Yes?"

He moved faster. "Are you sharing with me again tonight?"

"No, I don't think so," she said calmly. "You need your sleep to get better."

That wasn't good enough. He knew he'd sleep better with her beside him. He took her arm. "Jess, I want you to share my bed."

"That's very flattering, but I can't tonight."

"Why not?"

They had almost reached his bedroom door. She

turned fully around and looked up at him. "I can't, Steve. We're not destined to be together. In a week or two, you'll be back in L.A., being an undercover drug agent, and I'll be here, in Rawhide. I can't make a habit of sleeping with you, because I'd miss you too much when you're gone."

"Twice is making a habit of it?"

She dropped her gaze. "I'm afraid so. But don't worry, you'll be safe."

"Damn it, Jess! I'm not worried about my safety. I just want—I want to hold you again." He hated admitting the weakness he'd discovered, but if it made a difference in her decision, then admitting his need for her would be worth it.

He thought he saw a response in her eyes before she shuttered them. "I'll be back in a minute."

Relief flooded him. He'd have one more night and morning with Jess. The world would disappear and he'd be safe and happy here in Rawhide.

Waiting patiently in the hallway, he saw her door open and straightened, ready to hold her again.

Jessica emerged from her bedroom with Murphy at her heels. If he had to take the dog to get Jessica, he'd do it. He smiled and held out his arms.

"Murphy is going to sleep in your room tonight to be sure no one disturbs your rest."

He stared at her. She couldn't be serious. Murphy wasn't what he wanted. "Jess, you don't understand!"

"I told you before I have a superior brain, Steve Carter. I know what you want, but you need to stay strong and concentrate on the next few days. I'm not going to sleep with you. But I won't leave you unprotected, either. If anyone comes in, yell. Now, I'm going to take Murphy into your room and explain everything to him."

"You're going to explain to the dog? Like you think he can understand?" Steve said derisively.

"Yes. Excuse me." She shoved past him and opened his door, motioning for Murphy to follow her. "Come on in, Steve."

What choice did he have? He walked into his bedroom. "Okay, now what?"

"Murphy, guard." Then she turned to leave.

"That's it? That's the discussion?"

"There's no need for anything else. Good night." She left him, closing the door behind her.

Murphy woofed gently, as if to remind him to move. Steve absently patted the dog's head. Then, with a sigh, he stripped, turned off the light and got in the bed, pulling the covers up.

Suddenly something landed on the bed with a thud. Murphy had joined him.

"Hey, boy, aren't you supposed to sleep on the floor?"

Murphy ignored him and dug under the covers,

turned around and laid down, his head all that was visible.

"Okay. I guess we're stuck with each other." He settled down beside Murphy, just a pair of guys together for the night.

JESSICA HAD PLANNED TO rise early and let Steve sleep late that morning. However, after a restless night, without both Steve and Murphy to warm her bed, she'd awoken hours after she'd intended.

Fortunately, last night she'd divided up the tasks she needed done the next day among her aunts, her mother and her cousin Patience.

The kitchen was completely empty when Jessica finally entered it. But when Red and Mildred heard Jess pouring herself a cup of coffee, they appeared out of the back bedroom.

"Well, there's our sleeping beauty," Red said with a grin. "We thought you'd taken up Hollywood ways and would be sleeping until noon."

"Come on, Red, it's not that late," Jessica protested with a grin. "It's not even ten o'clock yet."

Mildred ignored her husband's teasing. She heated up a cinnamon roll and put it in front of Jessica.

"Bless you, Mildred," Jessica said, inhaling the cinnamon scent. "I'm hungry, I'll have to admit."

"Where's that boy of yours?" Red asked. "I don't want to have to cook two different breakfasts."

"He's a man, Red, not a boy." And she should know, after their one incredible night together. Before she flushed from the memory, she got up from the table. "I'll go wake him up. You'd better heat up another cinnamon roll, Mildred. I know he's going to want one."

She ran up the stairs to Steve's room, knocked and opened the door.

Murphy greeted her with a woof. But there was no sign of Steve. She petted her dog. "Where's Steve, Murphy? Did he run away?"

"No, he didn't," Steve said from the door. "I was just taking a shower." He was wearing a clean T-shirt and warm-up pants and socks. "It would be kind of difficult to run away without shoes," he said, nodding to the pair beside the bed.

"True. You'd better hurry. Mildred and Red are making your breakfast."

"I'm ready."

"Did you sleep all right?"

He gave her a level look. "Surprisingly well, thank you. And you?"

"No. I missed Murphy," she said and walked out of his room, the dog at her heels.

When they entered the kitchen, Red was putting their plates on the table.

"I fixed you a smaller breakfast this morning because you need a big appetite for lunch," Red said.

Steve stared at the loaded plate in front of him. "Lunch? I won't be able to eat lunch. Not after this."

"You have to, boy. We're fixing barbecue. You can't skip that."

Steve fought the urge to eat faster so he'd be ready for that mouth-watering lunch. "It's a good thing I don't have any of my old pants because I don't think I'd fit into them."

Jessica smiled. "It's a new form of torture. They cook the greatest meals in the world, and we all have to watch our weight."

"Now, missy, you don't have any problem with that," Red said. "You need more meat on your bones. They must have not fed you well in California."

"The film adds ten pounds, Red. I had to stay thin."

"I think you look perfect."

At Steve's remark, Jessica almost choked on her eggs. She glanced up at him and saw him rake his eyes down her body, seated next to him.

The few seconds of ensuing silence felt like a lifetime. Why didn't Red or Mildred say something? She certainly couldn't.

Thankfully, at that moment they heard a vehicle coming down the driveway.

Red went to the window. "It looks like Patience and Janie are back."

"Oh, good. I hope they got everything."

Steve stopped eating. "What were they supposed to get?"

"You some clothes. Jeans, coat, shirt, boots and a belt with a cowboy buckle. Hmm, I think that was all."

"You mean I get to wear real clothes? Hallelujah!"

"You're not going to wear the clothes today. You'll just try them on and then we'll wash them so they won't look so new."

"Even the boots?"

"No, those you need to wear and scuff them up a little if you can."

"I'll go outside and—"

"Absolutely not. You have to stay in the house, remember?" Since the shooting incident, neither of them had gone outside. Jessica had to admit even she was going stir-crazy. But the precaution was necessary. "You'll get to leave in the morning," she reminded him.

When the two women arrived at the back door with their arms full, Steve leaped to his feet and took some of the excess packages from them. "Where are we taking these things?" he asked Jessica.

"Right here." She cleared the table for the packages. "Show us what you bought."

Patience said, "Sarah said any time we want to have a shopping spree, we're welcome at her shop."

"Yes, it was fun. Here, how's this?" Janie asked, pulling out a light blue shirt with snaps.

"Oh, that's perfect. It will make his blue eyes show up more." Jessica held it up to Steve. "What do you think?"

"It's okay. Why does it have snaps instead of buttons?"

"That's what a lot of cowboys wear if they don't have wives to sew on the lost buttons," Janie teased.

"Oh. Yeah, it's fine."

"Here are your boots, Steve. They're work boots instead of cowboy boots. I hope that's okay."

He took them from Patience and sat down to pull them on. "They feel good," he said, standing up and moving about the kitchen.

"You'll need to take those off and go try on the jeans with the shirt. If they both fit, we'll get them in the wash," Jessica said. Then she opened another sack. "Oh, this is perfect."

Steve paused, staring at the scrap of denim she pulled out of the bag. "What is that?"

"The skirt I'm going to wear."

Steve stared at it. "That can't possibly cover your—" He stopped as he realized everyone in the room was staring at him. "I mean, it's a little short, isn't it?"

"I certainly hope so," Jessica said sweetly, holding it to her waist. "I want to attract attention, remember?"

"Yeah, but—"

"Go try on your clothes." After he left the room, she looked at the two shoppers. "You've done well so far. What about the coat?"

"It's here. Sarah had one that had been returned and it has a few scuff marks on it." Janie looked at Jessica. "We thought that would be something you'd want. She gave us a discount."

"Perfect," Jessica said.

The door opened and Steve came in wearing the stiff jeans and the snap shirt. "These jeans are a little long," he complained.

"Put on your boots and we'll show you why," Jessica assured him.

After staring at her, he did as she said.

"Now, see how your jeans stack? Cowboys like to have their jeans long so they'll stack on top of the boots."

"Okay, you're the authority, but the ends of the jeans will get dirty."

"We know," Janie said with a chuckle. "We're the ones who wash them."

"Try on this jacket over your clothes," Jessica said, holding it out for him to slip his arms into it.

"This is nice. And it's warm. I won't get cold in this thing."

"Too bad you can't wear a cowboy hat," Jessica said with a sigh.

"Why can't I?"

"Because it would hide your hair, and I want it to be seen."

"You're not still thinking about putting blond tips in my hair?"

"Of course I am. It's part of your disguise," she said with a big smile. She turned to Patience and Janie. "Did you talk to Betty Jean?"

"We did," Janie said. "She's coming this afternoon. And she agreed to loan you her driver's license too."

"We even talked to Howard Hensen," Patience added. "Mike had already called him. He not only loaned you his license, but he sent you his senior ring and his letter jacket, so everything would be authentic." She pulled them both out of the last bag.

"That's wonderful! I was a little worried about using Casey's. Now the right name is on the jacket. Look, Steve. It's perfect," Jessica said in excitement.

"You're wearing that coat?"

"Yes." She slipped her arms in it as Patience held it out. "I'll be warm, too."

"And since it won't cover your skirt, so will every man who sees you in it." Steve didn't sound happy.

"I hope so," Jessica replied, still smiling. "Now go change so we can wash these clothes."

Steve marched out of the room, clearly irritated.

WHEN BETTY JEAN HUNT arrived that afternoon, she carried in a lot of supplies. "I hope I brought everything you need."

"It looks like you brought the entire shop," Jessica said with a grin.

Her mother and Aunt Megan had returned from Buffalo a little earlier, and Steve was in one of the bathrooms putting in the blue contacts they'd bought for him.

Among the things they'd bought for Jessica was a push-up bra and a spandex top that would reveal her décolletage. They'd brought a chain that would make Howard's senior ring fall just where it would emphasize her low neckline.

"Let's start with me. Steve's not quite ready yet."

"Okay, but I'm dying to get a look at him. I've heard he's a hunk."

Jessica fought back the urge to tell Betty Jean that Steve was *her* hunk. Instead she said, "Yes, he is." Then she went into detail about what she wanted done to her hair.

When Betty Jean finished an hour later, Jessica was a blonde with lots of curls, just like her hairdresser.

When she emerged from her bedroom and returned to the kitchen, everyone stared at her.

"I can't believe it's you, honey," Anna said.

Jessica smiled. "It's me. And it's only a rinse.

It'll fade away in a few days." She looked around the room. "Where's Steve?"

"He's in the living room walking around in his boots, making sure he's broken them in." Red looked at Jessica. "Have you seen the blue contacts?"

"No, I haven't. Do they look good?"

"Yeah," Anna said. "It really makes a difference."

About that time, Steve walked into the kitchen. Jessica waited for him to comment about her hair.

He spoke to Red, almost not noticing her. Then he said, "I don't think I've met— Jess!"

"Hi, blue eyes. How are you doing?"

"Fine." He kept staring at her hair.

"Betty Jean is ready for you now. Come on, I'll introduce you."

"Are you sure this is necessary?"

"Oh, yes, Steve, I'm sure. Come on." Jessica left the kitchen, hoping he'd follow.

In the bedroom where Betty Jean had set up shop, she greeted Steve with an enthusiastic once-over. "Oh, yes, you sure do live up to your billing. Come sit down."

She stood behind him and ran her hands through his hair. "Now, Jess, you're sure you want a botched job on his hair? I can make it look good."

"I know, Betty Jean, but I want it to look like an amateur did it. It's important for our disguises."

"How will you get out of here?" Betty Jean asked, avid interest in her voice.

Steve said nothing.

Jessica said, "I'm sorry, Betty Jean, but we can't talk about it. I'll tell you all about it when I get back."

"He's not coming back?" Betty Jean asked, looking wistfully at Steve.

"I'm not sure. It's up to him, but he works in L.A., you know."

"Mmm, I envy you, Jess, going to Hollywood. Was it wonderful?"

"In some ways. In others, Rawhide beats it by a country mile," Jessica assured a disbelieving Betty Jean.

Half an hour later, after Betty Jean trimmed his hair slightly and dyed blond tips in it, she then greased it up and spiked it.

"Betty Jean, that is exactly what I wanted. You've done an incredible job!" Jessica said. "Look, Steve. You might not recognize yourself, either."

"No, I wouldn't," he replied, looking in the mirror. "Will mine wash out, too?"

"Uh, no, but you can get those tips cut off right away. Your hair probably grows fast," Betty Jean said, not wanting to upset Steve.

"Don't worry. He'll survive because you did such a good job."

Jessica was eager to get Betty Jean on her way, minus her driver's license. She still wanted to try on her outfit to see if it worked like she thought it would, but she'd felt she had to keep Steve company while Betty Jean worked on him.

As Betty Jean headed for the door, Jessica encouraged Steve to come to the kitchen with them. "I want everyone to see your hair."

"I don't!" he growled.

"Don't be a spoilsport, Steve. And you really ought to thank Betty Jean."

"Yeah, thanks, Betty Jean."

"When you come back I'll cut them off for you free of charge," Betty Jean offered. She was definitely flirting with him, Jessica decided. And Steve didn't seem to mind.

"I might take you up on that offer if I get back here."

"I won't forget," she promised, a big smile on her face.

"I'm sure you won't," Jessica muttered under her breath.

"What did you say?" Betty Jean asked.

"I said, you certainly won't," she said quickly. "After all, you always had the best memory of anyone I know."

"That's true. Well, I'm off. Good luck whenever you go."

"Thanks," Steve said.

He hung back, not entering the kitchen until after Betty Jean had gone. And not until Jessica prodded him.

Brett Randall was by the table, having a drink. He swallowed hard and shook his head.

"Damn, son, anyone who'd go out looking like that has to be brave. At least now I won't worry about you."

But Steve was worried. Very worried.

Jessica's plan sounded good, looked good on paper, but would some clothes and hair dye be enough to fool some desperate agents?

FROM HIS POSITION HIGH in the tree, Baldwin had a great view of the back door of the ranch house. He'd been there all night, waiting for his opportunity.

But Steve hadn't reappeared.

He kept his rifle in his hand, ready for a quick shot, if that was all he got. But as the hours passed, he couldn't help thinking his efforts were futile. He was hungry, tired and he had to pee again. Was Carter even still in there? Was he ever planning to come out, or was he too busy bedding the redhead?

Maybe he should abandon this stakeout. Get in his truck and head back to L.A. He'd call his wife and tell her to meet him at the airport with their passports, money and her jewels. He wouldn't leave them behind, not after he'd worked so hard to pay for them. In hours they could be on a beach in Mexico, or someplace he'd be safe.

Safe from Miguel?

He scoffed at his own stupidity. No one would ever be safe from Miguel Antonio. His boss would never get off the gravy train of dirty drug deals that made him millions. And Baldwin knew too much for Miguel to let him simply walk away.

As if on cue his cell phone vibrated. Whispering, even though he was way out of earshot of anyone on the ranch, Baldwin said, "Yeah?"

"Is it done?" It was Miguel. Checking up on his progress.

"Not yet. But I know where he's hiding." As if that meant anything.

Miguel cursed and his tone became menacing. "I want it done today."

"Yes, sir."

"Just in case you lose him again," he said sarcastically, "I've put agents at all the airports in Wyoming and the surrounding states. We'll get him. We have to. Or we're all screwed." Miguel laughed, a dark laugh meant to scare Baldwin. "If we don't, I'll get *you*."

Miguel succeeded. Baldwin snapped shut his phone. Just as he'd thought, there was only one way for this to end.

He picked up his rifle and lined up the back door of the ranch in his scope, dead center.

It was the perfect shot.

Now all he needed was Steve Carter to emerge.

Chapter Twelve

It was a short night.

The latest they could leave for the airport in Denver was four in the morning.

When Steve stumbled into the kitchen, wearing real clothes for the first time since he'd arrived in Rawhide, his hair lay flat on his head.

"Steve, you didn't fix your hair," Jessica said at once.

But he hadn't heard a word. He was staring at her, his mouth open. He hadn't seen her in her disguise before. The skirt that he'd seen yesterday rode on her hips and barely covered her rear. And her top was spandex, bright red, dipping low in front.

Steve had no complaints about Jessica's body. But he hadn't remembered her being that well-endowed. He couldn't take his eyes off her.

"Jess, you can't— You need to put something on!"

"Exactly what I told her!" Brett said.

"But you have to admit it's distracting, right?" Jessica asked brightly.

His gaze was still on the mounds of her breasts. "That shirt doesn't even meet with your skirt!"

"And you're from Los Angeles?" Jessica teased. "Everyone bares their skin there."

All Steve could do was shake his head.

"I've tried talking to her," Brett said. "All she says is it's part of your disguise. I expect you to take care of her, Steve. You hear me?"

Anna patted her husband's arm. "I suspect everyone hears you, dear. Remember some family members are trying to sleep."

"Red made us some coffee and egg and sausage biscuits for the drive. Are you ready to go?" Jessica asked. "Did you tape the envelope to your chest?"

"Of course. That's what this trip is all about."

Brett and Jake stood up from the table. "Okay, we're going to back out the truck in front of the house. You two come out the front door and get in the back seat and stay low, so you can't be seen."

Jess nodded at her father.

Anna hugged her husband goodbye, as did B.J., each warning her husband to be careful. Then they both hugged Jessica and Steve. After the men went outside, Jessica and Steve went to the front door. Beside it was a blanket and a pillow.

"What are those for?" Steve asked.

"Things to make the ride more comfortable for you."

"I'm not a baby," Steve growled.

"I know," Jessica said, picking up the blanket and pillow. They heard the truck and opened the door slightly. The cold air rushed in.

When the truck came into view, Steve and Jessica rushed out into the open door.

As Brett moved it forward, Jake said over his shoulder, "We should be to Tori's house in about fifteen minutes. When we get there, we'll pull into the garage. Then we'll get out and get in Tori's car."

They made the ride in silence.

At Tori's, they switched cars, then drove through Rawhide and headed toward Denver.

"Dad, if we're stopped, you just tell the cops you're going to the airport to pick up a part for your computer, and Howie and I asked for a ride since we're going on vacation. Okay?"

Brett looked at Jake. "You think that's a possibility?" he asked.

"I don't know. But it's best to be prepared. Right, Betty Jean?"

Jessica assumed her life-or-death role. "Right, Mr. Randall."

Wasting no time, she pulled out from her purse the jar of hair gel Betty Jean had used on Steve and spiked his hair.

Steve capitulated, but he made disgusted sounds that made him resemble a growling dog.

When she had his hair standing on end, she wiped her hands and passed out the breakfast and coffee.

When they'd all finished, Jessica suggested Steve use the pillow to get some sleep.

"Why me? Are you going to sleep?"

"No, but I haven't sustained a bullet wound recently," Jessica pointed out.

"I'm fine."

Jessica frowned at him. He was being difficult and it was going to be a long day. She knew—

They all heard the siren at the same time.

"Looks like you were right, honey," Brett muttered.

"I always am, *Mr. Randall,*" she said, emphasizing his name to remind him of their roles.

"Good morning, folks," the deputy said as soon as Brett rolled down his window after coming to a stop.

"Is there a problem, Officer?" Brett asked.

"I need to see your license and registration, sir."

Brett handed them out. After he studied them, the officer looked at the others. "Do all of you have identification?" At their nod, he asked, "May I see them, please?"

Brett passed them through the window. "Officer, I'm not trying to be difficult, but what's going on?"

"We're looking for a suspect and I've been ordered to check all IDs."

He scanned their licenses. Then he looked at Steve. "Sir, this doesn't look like you."

Jessica didn't wait for Steve to answer.

"Well, it did, but I thought he looked kind of boring. So, for our vacation, I insisted he let me change his hairstyle. Doesn't he look good? I have a beauty shop in Rawhide. I'll give you a discount if you come in. You can look like him, too." Jessica beamed at the deputy.

Brett looked over the back seat. "Yeah, Howie, lean forward and let the man see that special do of yours." He laughed after he said it.

"It looks really good, Mr. Randall!" Jessica protested.

The officer handed back their IDs. "Okay, folks, sorry I delayed you."

"No problem," Brett said and rolled up his window. Then he pulled back onto the road and sped away.

"How did you know we'd be stopped?" he asked his daughter a few minutes later.

"I wasn't sure, but I was stopped twice trying to get away. Once was in L.A. and then again in Wyoming."

"Well, thanks for warning us, Jess," her father said. "But it should be free sailing now."

From beside her, Steve added in a somber voice, "Until we get to the airport."

AS STEVE HAD PREDICTED, their IDs were checked at the airport just to enter the parking lot. Jake and Brett went into the airport with them, but Jessica warned her father not to hug her or kiss her goodbye. "Remember, I'm just an acquaintance from Rawhide."

"Okay, Betty Jean. I'll remember."

"Good," she said with a grin as she slipped her arms into the letter jacket. She arranged the coat so that her chest was prominently displayed. She reached over for Steve, who had donned his leather jacket with the sheepskin lining.

"Here we go, Howie," she said and reached up to kiss him.

"People are staring," Steve muttered under his breath.

"Good." She nuzzled his neck. "Uncle Jake is carrying our suitcase. Can you take it from him?"

"Suitcase? What suitcase?"

"I put it in the truck last night. People would be suspicious if we didn't take luggage on a vacation. Don't worry. It doesn't have anything that I need. We won't bother with it when we get to the airport in D.C."

"You're just going to walk away and leave it?"

"Yes. Can you carry it? It will look strange if you don't."

"Sure." Then in a louder voice he said, "Here, Mr. Randall, I can take that bag. Thanks for getting it out of the trunk for us."

"Not a problem, Howie. You and Betty Jean have a good vacation."

Steve shook Jake's hand and then Brett's.

"We'll see you when you get back, Howie," Brett said. "You and Betty Jean," he added, his gaze intense.

"Yes, sir. I hope to see you soon."

Jessica wrapped her hand around Steve's arm. It kept her from hugging her father. "Come on, Howie. We've got to check in."

Jessica and Steve got in line to check their one bag and pick up their tickets. Jessica had reserved the tickets yesterday with Betty Jean's credit card, after giving her friend a check to cover the charge.

When they reached the counter, Jessica showed her license and Betty Jean's credit card. Steve gave the agent Howie's license.

When the agent looked at Steve, Jessica said, "I changed his hair for our vacation. Doesn't he look cool?" she asked. "I did it in my salon. Everyone was jealous. I'll probably have a jillion appointments when I get back." She beamed at the woman, as if expecting her to praise Howie's hair.

"It—it certainly looks different," the woman said, shoving Howie's license back to him.

After a couple of minutes, she handed over their tickets and tagged their bag, putting it on the luggage conveyer belt. "You may go straight to your gate now. You've got about forty-five minutes before boarding."

"Thank you! We're so excited about our vacation," Jessica said as she pushed back her jacket, exposing more of her body to everyone they passed.

Steve moved closer. "Don't you think you should tone it down a little?"

She snuggled up to him. "Didn't you see those men in dark suits staring at everyone? I think they could be government agents."

"They are. I even know a couple of them."

She made sure to breathe through the tightness that gripped her chest. "So, it's proof our disguises are good, then."

"Well, yours certainly is."

She stretched up to kiss him, as if he'd said something incredibly sweet. "Oh, we are going to have so much fun!"

She hung on his arm until they reached the security gate.

Jessica waltzed through with no problem, but behind her, Steve set off the buzzer.

The security agent stepped forward with the wand. "Sir, please remove your belt buckle."

He did, set it on the conveyer that went through

the X-ray machine, then walked through the sensors without further incident.

"Oh, Howie," Jessica gushed when he came through, "I'm so glad you made it." She kissed him again.

"You're overdoing it," he whispered. Then he wrapped an arm around her and moved forward. "Where's our gate?"

"It's number ten, right down here," Jessica said quietly.

"They'll be watching all the flights to D.C.," Steve pointed out.

"Of course. Ooh, Howie, when we get to D.C., can we go to George Washington's home? It's called Mount…Mount something. Mount Washington?"

"I think that would be Mount Vernon," Steve muttered, rolling his eyes.

"That's right, Mount Vernon. I've heard it's great and we can take a ride on the river, too."

"The Potomac."

"Silly, I knew the name of the river," Jessica announced with a delighted giggle that had heads turning. She tucked her arm into his and snuggled closer as they walked. Her coat, as if by accident, slid a little more open.

They reached their gate and looked for a couple of seats.

"Over here, Howie," Jessica said, having found

two seats about five chairs apart. "Could you please move down so my sweetie and I can sit together?"

"No, Betty Jean," Steve protested.

"It's all right, honey, they don't mind. Just scoot down two more," she pleaded, bending down to ask one reluctant man. "Aren't you a dear!" she exclaimed when he did as she asked.

After settling in and crossing her legs in her short skirt, she turned to those around her. "We're going on vacation! I'm so excited!"

Several of the men leaned forward so they could have a better view of Jessica in all her glory. Steve kept an eye on her, but he didn't contribute to the conversation.

Jessica knew he'd noticed the dark-suited man who moved through the waiting area. His eyes, she saw, flitted around the gate from one agent to another. She turned to him, giving him another kiss, trying to draw him into the character.

She continued her conversation with the men around her, not looking at the suited gentleman until he pushed his way past her.

"Oh, sorry I got in your way," she said sarcastically.

The man looked down at her. "Excuse me," he muttered and kept on going.

"Well! Some people!" Then she returned to her audience. "Do we get a meal on the plane? I'm starving." Turning to Steve, after the men said they wouldn't be serving them much, she said, "Howie, honey, do you think you could go buy me a snack for the trip? And maybe a Diet Coke?" When he agreed, she leaned in and gave him another kiss. "Thank you, sweetie."

She watched Steve walk over to one of the airport restaurants before she turned back to the other men. "Isn't he the sweetest thing? He takes good care of me."

Then she began asking about what to see in D.C. and struggled not to stare after Steve, which would give away her concern. When he settled down in his seat again, she turned around. "What did you bring me?"

He gave her a can of Diet Coke and a wrapped sandwich.

"Oh, you got my favorite, Howie." She beamed at him. "Did you get something for yourself? You need to keep your strength up, you know." She chuckled. "For later," she added, and watched Steve flush.

"Uh, yeah, I got a snack." He held up a bag of chips.

When the gate agent announced the beginning of boarding, Jessica pouted.

"Oh! I haven't finished, Howie. Will you hold my Diet Coke while I wrap up my sandwich?"

"Yeah, but you'd better hurry. We're in the first seating because we're in the back of the plane."

"I wish we could've afforded first class. That would be a lot of fun," she said longingly.

"Maybe another time," Steve muttered.

"Excuse me," a stern, masculine voice asked, interrupting their private moment. "Are you going to D.C.?"

Jessica looked up, straight into the dark eyes of a government agent.

Chapter Thirteen

Her heart was pounding, her mouth suddenly dry.
Here it was—the biggest challenge of her disguises.
She resisted the urge to reach out for Steve and in-
stead she let herself fall once again into character.
She was Betty Jean Hunt, a hairdresser from Raw-
hide, Wyoming.

Jessica beamed at the man. "Oh, yes. We're on vacation. I've never seen the capitol before."

"Well, I don't think you should take your leftover
food on the plane. They've been having trouble with
that."

What? That was why he'd come to them—to
warn her about bringing food on the plane?

Still, the man's gaze seemed fixed on Steve.

She played up her naiveté. "Really? I didn't know
that. Howie thought it would be all right."

"This is Howie?" the man asked.

"Yes, of course." She handed Steve her sandwich

and soda can. "Will you throw these away for me, please?"

The man stopped him. "You know, I could be wrong. Why don't you ask the flight attendant before you throw it out?"

"Okay, I will," Jess assured him. As the suited man turned to leave, she exchanged a look of relief with Steve.

JESSICA HAD HOPED they would be safe once they got on the plane. She'd snagged a little pillow for Steve and encouraged him to take the window seat. Then she told him to take off his jacket. Once he settled against the pillow, she covered him with his coat.

After slipping off the letter jacket she was wearing, she buckled her seat belt and turned to the man on the other side of her. "Isn't this exciting?"

Prepared to bury his nose in a newspaper, the man looked up in surprise. His gaze focused on Jessica's chest and it took several seconds before he answered her question. "Isn't what exciting?"

"Flying! I've only flown once before." She went into great detail about her supposed first flight, which lasted until after the plane had taken off.

Once the seat belt sign had been turned off, Jessica noted that several of the dark suits were on board and prowled up and down the aisles, reexamining all of the faces. She was glad Steve was getting some sleep and glad he was presenting an un-concerned front.

She also noticed that she drew the gaze of the men as they went past, which was exactly what she'd intended. But the most severe test was ahead of them. Getting into the proper building would be difficult, even with an appointment.

There would be people there who knew Steve well.

It was unfortunate that he hadn't been able to bring a gun. But they would be looking for anyone who notified the airlines that he had a permit to carry a weapon.

No, they were dependent on their wits…and their disguises.

Jessica kept up the chatter the entire flight, even though she wanted to sleep. The lack of sleep was catching up with her. She would occasionally look at Steve, glad he was getting the rest but wishing she could join him.

When the plane began its descent, she turned her back on her companion, much to his disappointment, to awaken Steve. "Howie, it's time to wake up."

He had been deeply asleep, but he was used to danger. Steve knew immediately where he was…and who he was supposed to be. "Oh, hi, Betty Jean. Did I fall asleep?"

"Yes, Howie, you slept the entire trip, but the plane's starting to land and I need you to hold my hand. You know how scared I am when the plane is landing."

"I know, honey," he agreed, sitting up.

"Oh, you flattened your hair." She reached up and spiked his hair again. "I want everyone to see your hair. It's so cool."

"Here, give me your hand because we're going to land," Steve said, reaching out to hold her hand.

She snuggled up to him, thinking how easy this acting job was. There had been times in Hollywood where she had to pretend warmth toward men she detested. Pretending interest in Steve was hardly acting.

"Oh, Howie, you take such good care of me." She lay her head on his shoulder.

He whispered in her ear. "Did the suits come by while I slept?"

"Of course. I entertained them."

"I bet you did," he growled.

"Oh, Howie, you're so sweet," she said, kissing him again.

"You know, I could get used to that," he whispered.

"What?"

He said nothing at first, just turned and kissed her lips. "That."

"You've done such a good job, Howie, I didn't even notice when we landed," she told him.

"Good. You'd better make sure you have everything you brought on board."

"Right." It was time for the big test.

The man on the other side of Jessica wanted to tell her goodbye, and she thanked him for entertaining her so she wasn't so nervous on her flight.

"Good thing we're here," Steve whispered, "or he'd be drooling soon."

She elbowed him in the stomach as he stood, throwing a challenging smile over her shoulder. They filed out when it was their turn, but as they progressed toward the exit door, Jessica saw two dark suits standing with the flight attendants, watching the passengers file out.

Jessica breathed deeply and painted a bright smile on her face while she made sure her jacket was open enough to draw attention. When they reached the door, she smiled at the cabin crew. "Thank you so much for making our flight so nice. It's a perfect start for our vacation."

She let her smile drift to the two men in dark suits as she reached for Steve's hand. "Come on, Howie, I can't wait!"

Steve came after her, saying nothing.

When the long hall fed into the waiting room and the rest of the airport, they discovered another few men in dark suits. Jessica slipped off her coat. "It's warm in here, isn't it?"

"Yeah," Steve agreed, but he kept his coat on.

Forcing herself to continue to act like an excited young woman on vacation, she wrapped herself around Steve's arm as they followed the crowd toward the baggage claim area.

"Are we waiting for our bag?" Steve asked softly.

"No, but if we rush out now, we'll call attention to ourselves." Then she raised her voice and said, "Oh, look, Howie. Isn't this exciting?"

"So much so I don't think I can stand it," Steve whispered wryly.

They passed another agent as they moved toward the exit. "Let's look at the luggage for a minute," Jessica said with a whisper. When the man next to her pulled a couple of bags off the carousel, Jessica spoke to him, as if they were old friends. Then, when the man turned to leave, she grabbed Steve's arm and followed the man out to the taxi stand, where there was a line of people waiting for a cab.

"I hate standing in line," she whispered to Steve.

"Yeah. It's a dangerous thing with all these agents wandering around."

When someone got in the line behind them, Jessica switched to her Betty Jean persona, bubbling over about their vacation.

Steve gave her a strange look until he looked over his shoulder and saw the agent standing behind them. He gave the man a smile and rolled his blue eyes as Jessica continued to talk nonstop.

She pulled him back around to get his attention, telling him what she wanted them to do on their vacation, including spending a few lazy mornings in bed.

"Betty Jean," Steve muttered, "people can hear you."

The agent behind him said, "Don't worry, son. They'll all be jealous."

"Maybe so, but I get embarrassed," Steve said.

"I think the man is right. Everyone will be jealous," Jessica said with pouty lips, leaning toward Steve.

As the line edged slowly to the waiting taxis, the man behind them asked where they were going.

Fortunately, Jessica had prepared for that question and she named a hotel near the building that housed the DEA.

"That's close to where I'm going. Mind if I share your cab?"

Jessica swallowed a protest and said, "Of course not. That would be fine. We're in no hurry," she assured him. "Where are you going?"

He named their ultimate destination, and Jessica did the best acting she'd ever done. "And you say that's near our hotel?"

"Sure is. I work near there."

"Oh, so you were on vacation?"

"No, little lady, My trip was business. My car is

parked at my office, so this will work out just fine. I'll be glad to contribute to your vacation money," he added with a grin.

"Well, isn't that neighborly of you," she answered with a big smile.

Another cab pulled up and the three of them got in, Jessica in the middle.

"Where to?" the cabbie asked over his shoulder.

The agent gave him his destination, then added their hotel.

Along the way Jessica played tourist, asking their companion about everything she saw. He answered her questions, but he kept bringing Steve into the conversation. Jessica worried the man would recognize Steve's voice.

When the taxi stopped by the building where his car was parked, the agent took out a twenty. "Here. This should cover the fare to your hotel. Thanks for sharing."

They both thanked him as he got out of the cab. Then, as the cabbie pulled away, she drew a deep breath of relief.

Jessica leaned forward to the cabbie. "Sir, we don't want to go to that hotel. Can you just drive us around town for the next hour and a half and then end up right back here about a quarter to two?"

The cabbie frowned. "You want to see all the famous buildings or something?"

"Yes," Jessica agreed, "but if we fall asleep, don't wake us until you get back here at 1:45."

"That's going to run up a big bill. You sure you can pay it?"

She opened her purse and pulled out a hundred-dollar bill. "Take this as down payment. If it's more than that, we're good for it."

"What are you doing?" Steve muttered.

"Renting us a safe place to catch a nap," Jessica whispered, settling her head on his shoulder.

STEVE DIDN'T GO TO SLEEP.

He put his arm around Jessica and let her relax against his body and lay his head atop hers. It was a sweet feeling as he felt her go to sleep, trusting him to protect her. For so much of the time they'd spent together she had been the one to protect him.

He'd never met a woman like her.

She'd gone to Hollywood—Sin City, her father called it—conquered it, and then she'd chosen to return home, giving up a promising movie career. She'd faced threats, even death, and still refused to let him disappear.

Jessica Randall was an outstanding woman.

He didn't want to let her go.

She'd told him she wasn't asking for promises. But for the first time in his life he wanted to give them. For the first time in his life he wanted a future.

But he couldn't promise her anything.

After today, *if* he managed to get to the office of the head of the DEA and convince him of what he believed, he'd be required to help clean up the mess in L.A. And Los Angeles was a long way from Wyoming.

Even afterward, he couldn't go to Wyoming. He was an undercover drug-enforcement agent. He didn't think they had a big drug problem in Wyoming. What could he do to support a wife and maybe even children in Rawhide?

He pulled the slumbering Jessica a little closer to him. He hated the idea of letting her go with him into the building. Even though he knew her disguise had worked for him all day, he didn't want her to be put at risk.

His immediate boss, Miguel Antonio, wouldn't hesitate to kill Jessica in order to avoid capture and conviction. He must have become hardened to the good side of himself if the theft of drugs had gone on as long as Steve feared it had. Jessica, if Miguel tried to kill her, wouldn't be the first who had died to ensure he wasn't discovered.

"Sir?" the cabbie asked suddenly, pulling Steve from his thoughts. "You wish me to continue?"

"Yes," Steve agreed. "Just make sure to get us back to that address by 1:45."

"Okay. Here's the Lincoln Memorial," he pointed out, looking in the mirror at Steve.

"Yeah, I've seen it."

"You're not a first-time visitor?"

"Nope."

No, he wasn't a newcomer to D.C. or its politics. He wasn't sure what he would do if he couldn't convince the head of DEA, Mr. Walter Grouse. Steve had met the man several times, but Miguel was the fair-haired boy around there, second in command for Grouse.

Grouse might refuse to believe him.

He'd have to make Grouse believe the evidence. He couldn't let Miguel continue to spread the sadness that was the result of drugs. Families devastated, parents losing hope because they couldn't help their children get off the drugs, or babies born with crack already in their systems.

That was why he had to succeed.

"We're going back now," the cabbie said, again rousing Steve from his thoughts.

He waited until they were almost there before he woke Jessica.

"Honey, we're here."

He watched as her heavy eyelids slowly moved upward. With a slightly dazed look that told him she didn't get nearly enough sleep, she said with a slight frown, "Where?"

"At the DEA," he said and gave her a quick kiss. Only to help her remember their personas, he told himself.

Jessica sat up and pulled out a compact from her large purse. She immediately put on more lipstick and combed the curls all over her head. Then she powdered her nose. "Okay, I'm ready." She turned to Steve and shot him a conspiratorial look.

"Do you think that nice man who rode with us will still be around there?" she asked. "He might think our appearance there is a little strange."

"Yeah, I'm sure he would. We can only hope he's gone home, like he said."

The cabbie stopped in the no-parking zone to allow his passengers direct access to the building.

"Do we owe you any more?" Jessica asked.

"No, ma'am. I owe you." The cabdriver began peeling off bills from a roll he had in his jacket.

"Keep it," she said with a smile. "It was a wonderful ride."

"But you slept the entire time," the cabbie protested.

"Yes, we did. And it was wonderful," she said and slipped out of the cab after Steve. "Wasn't it, Howie?"

"Sure," Steve agreed and let himself take one more kiss.

One of the two guards standing outside the doors muttered, "Who are these two lovebirds?"

"Tourists. They're probably lost," the other answered. He took a good look at Jessica. "I wouldn't mind being lost with her."

Jessica tugged on her skirt, which only emphasized its shortness, which was proved by the faces of the two guards. When they reached the door, she was wearing a big smile above her low neckline, and the two guards scarcely gave Steve a glance.

She told them about their appointment and the guards stepped aside, holding the doors open for them.

"Take the elevator on the left, ma'am," one of them called after Steve and Jessica. "Go to the top floor."

"All right, thank you," Jessica called with a wave.

Steve felt her hand wrapping around his arm.

"Not much longer," he whispered.

"I don't know why you insisted on coming here," Jessica complained, taking Steve by surprise. She'd lapsed once again into her Betty Jean character. "You could've probably gotten all the information off the Internet."

"Come on, Betty Jean," he said, getting into the spirit. "Since Dad arranged the interview, I kind of have to go."

"We could tell him we got lost. Then we could go to Mount Vernon. I hear it's so beautiful."

"But it's kind of cold today. I'm not sure my letter jacket would keep you warm enough."

"Well," she drawled, a sparkling look in her eyes, "we could cuddle enough to keep me warm."

He felt several people near them waiting for the elevator, but he didn't dare look around.

"You're embarrassing me, Betty Jean," he complained in a loud whisper.

She jerked her hand away and took a step back from him. Turning around to an older woman behind her, she complained, "Men are so difficult. At first, they want to make love all the time. Then, once they've got you under their spell, they're not interested."

"Betty Jean!" Steve protested in a sharp whisper.

"Well, it's true!"

Several men by the adjacent elevator chuckled.

At that moment, the elevator arrived. The doors slid open and several people exited. Steve slid behind Jessica to give them room. He breathed out slowly after the men had moved past them. One of them was Miguel Antonio, his boss.

"What's wrong?" Jessica whispered as they moved into the elevator.

"Later," he muttered. As they turned, the doors were closing and he saw Miguel turn around to stare right at him. He hoped he didn't recognize him.

In the elevator, Jessica, feeling his tension, began her routine again about them being on vacation and what she hoped to see. She asked everyone what they recommended they go see while in D.C.

Finally, one of the ladies asked, "What are you doing here?"

"Oh, my boyfriend promised his dad he'd come visit some guy he knows."

"Oh, I hate those kind of chores," the woman returned. Then the elevator opened on her floor and she got out.

Two floors later, the last person except for Steve and Jessica got out of the elevator.

When the doors closed, Jessica looked at Steve. "We're finally alone."

"Not to do what you have in mind," he said, staring straight ahead. "You've already embarrassed me enough." He hoped she understood what he was saying. He knew there were cameras and microphones in each elevator. He just hoped Miguel hadn't recognized him.

"Oh, you're just being difficult," she said with a pout. With her jacket pulled back, she put her hands on her hips and wiggled her body.

He figured whoever reviewed those tapes would keep them around for a long time. It certainly meant they wouldn't be looking at him. At least not yet.

Chapter Fourteen

The elevator doors slid open to a gracious area with lush carpet and furniture that looked comfortable but businesslike.

The only visible occupant was a middle-aged woman sitting behind a large desk with fresh flowers on it.

Steve took Jessica's hand and walked over to her. "We have an appointment to see Mr. Grouse."

Without even looking up, she said, "I'm sorry, Mr. Grouse is out of the office."

"No, he's not. Please let him know we're here."

The woman glared at Steve. "I'll do no such thing. I said he's out of the office."

"My father made the appointment. He'll be very disappointed to know that his old friend can't make time to meet me," Steve said. "The name is Howard Hensen."

"You're from out of town?"

"Yes."

"May I see some ID?"

Steve took his billfold out of his back jeans pocket and handed it over.

The woman examined it, then she stared at him. "This doesn't look like you."

"Well, no. I've grown some since that time, and my girlfriend—" he nodded toward Jessica "—decided to do my hair like this. I told you, Betty Jean, that no one would recognize me!"

"But you've got me along to tell 'em who you are, honey."

The woman looked at Jessica and asked stiffly, "Do you have ID?"

"Of course." She began digging in her big purse and the woman tapped her nails on the desk impatiently.

"Here it is," Jessica said, as if she expected to be praised for finally finding it. "Of course, my hair's not exactly the same color. After all, I *am* a hairstylist. Oh, I could do wonders with your hair. It would make you look so much…younger!" she said brightly.

"No, thank you. Just a moment."

The secretary got up and disappeared behind a door that had been closed.

"Howie, how long will this take?"

Steve looked at her, a sideways glance. "It will

take what it takes, Betty Jean. You'll just have to be patient."

She examined her nails. "Oh, no, I've nicked a nail. Now, where is that nail file? I'm sure it's in here." She dug around in her big purse but didn't come up with it before the door opened.

The woman came back out and gave each of them their IDs. "Mr. Grouse will see you for a minute. Then he'll get an agent to show you around."

When Steve and Jessica started toward the door, she said, "No! Wait here. He'll come out and shake your hands. Then you can take your tour."

"But I want to see his office," Jessica said and purposely moved around Steve to be closer to the door.

The woman began to object, "You can't—" But the door opened and an older man came out.

"Are you Mr. Grouse?" Jessica said in a sugary voice. "You are just the sweetest man to come greet us." She took his hand. Then she said, "Here's Howie. Howie Hensen. He's the one who really wanted to talk to you. Me, I'm just dying to see your office." As she made that last statement, she headed for the office Grouse had exited a second ago. "I want to tell the folks back home that you've got the best office of everyone," she announced as she entered.

"No! You can't go in there!" the secretary screamed and started after her.

"It's all right, Miss Carson. I'll take care of it." Mr. Grouse shook Steve's hand and said, "Shall we take a tour of my office, Mr. Hensen?"

"Yes, sir, thank you. Betty Jean doesn't mean to be pushy. It just seems to come naturally."

"I can believe that," he said as he and Steve entered his office.

"Oh, Mr. Grouse," Jessica called as soon as they came in. "You have such a wonderful view! Can you tell me what that building over there is? I think it might be the White House because it is white."

Since she was leaning forward and looking past the last window, Grouse had to cross the room to see where she was pointing.

Steve closed the door and then unsnapped his shirt so he could untape the evidence. At the unusual noise, Grouse spun around.

"What are you doing?" he demanded. "You can't close that door. That's not allowed." He began hurrying to the door.

"Wait!" Jessica called. "Mr. Grouse, this is Steve Carter, one of your undercover DEA agents."

Grouse looked at Steve. "No, it's not. I don't know what you're trying to pull, but Steve Carter was shot by drug dealers about ten days ago in Los Angeles. So you'd better come up with another scheme."

Steve took a step forward. "She's telling the truth,

sir, and I can prove it. If you open that door, my life is over. And maybe hers, too."

"Do you have a gun?" Grouse remained calm, his training evident.

Steve drew a deep breath. "No, sir, I don't. I knew they'd be looking for me at the airport. I didn't want to show my badge to be allowed to carry a gun."

"Is it really you, Carter?" Grouse stepped closer to look at him.

Steve nodded. "Yes, sir."

"Why would anyone be looking for you? Miguel told me you were dead."

"They were looking for me because Miguel had told them I was a turncoat, that I was selling drugs."

"You know this for a fact?"

"It's the only answer. He knew I had escaped the ambush he set up for me."

"How do you know that?"

"Because he's the only one I told of my suspicions about my partners."

"What suspicions?"

Steve said, "I'll show you what I found if you'll lock the door and be sure the intercom is turned off."

"You don't trust my secretary?" Grouse demanded.

"She first refused to admit us, telling us you were out of town. Then we had to convince her we were harmless before she'd let you know we were here and that we had an appointment."

They all three stood there in silence. Finally, Grouse walked to the door. Steve didn't know if he intended to lock the door or open it and walk out to his secretary.

When the man locked the door, Steve heard Jessica let out a big sigh of relief.

He smiled at her. Then he went to Grouse's desk and began laying out the information he'd gathered on his partners. Grouse sat down and let him explain the information. He showed him the pictures of the houses he had discovered in his partners' names and the amounts they had in their accounts.

"How can they afford this? They're not making that much money!" Grouse exclaimed.

Steve circled the desk and sat down in one of the chairs. "Come on, Jess, sit down."

She'd been silent the entire time. Now she crossed to the other chair and sat down beside him.

Grouse looked up at her. "Jess? I thought—"

"I'm Jessica Randall, Mr. Grouse. My father was the one who arranged the interview."

The man stared at Jessica, taking in her attire, before he said, "Brett Randall is a good man."

"Thank you. I think so, too." She added a sincere smile.

"If these men are doing what you say, Carter, they have to be stopped. I'll call Miguel and—"

"No!" Steve snapped. When Grouse raised his eyebrows, Steve said, "I've made that mistake once."

"What do you mean?"

"The night I was shot, I'd reported my suspicions to Miguel an hour before. My partners drilled me in the shoulder in a dark alley."

"You were actually shot?"

"Yes. Do you want to see the scar?"

"No. How did you survive?"

"Jessica opened her garage door just after I was shot and backed out into the alley. When she saw my body, she stopped her vehicle and came to see if I was alive."

Grouse's eyes widened as he looked at the fragile, feminine woman across from him. "That took guts, Miss Randall."

"It's what my daddy would've done, sir."

"Yes, it is. So she called the ambulance for you?"

"She intended to, but I told her it would mean my death. I managed to convince her not to call the police, either."

"How'd you do that?"

With a soft laugh, Steve said, "I don't really know."

"Young lady, can you explain it?"

Jessica shrugged. "I figured he had to be telling the truth if he was turning down help. So I took a chance on him."

"What did you do?"

"I put him in my SUV under all my clothes and got on a freeway until I was stopped by a highway patrolman. He said my SUV was similar to one used in a robbery and he wanted to search it. I told him he couldn't search because he'd mess up my clothes. I told him I was on my way to Texas. He let me go. I got off the freeway and headed north. Oh, and I changed my plates to my Wyoming plates."

"Did you take him all the way to Wyoming?"

"Yes. He was too injured to go anywhere on his own."

"What happened when you got him to…Rawhide, is it?"

"Yes, I turned him over to my brother-in-law and my cousin. They are the two doctors in Rawhide."

"Didn't they have to report the wound to the law?"

"Yes, that's Mike. He's my cousin-in-law."

"And when he recovered, you came with him to D.C.?"

Steve answered for her. "She did more than that. She killed one of my partners when he burst in with a gun and shot the place up." He sent a look of appreciation toward Jessica.

"I see," Grouse said, but he was frowning.

Steve continued. "And she devised our disguises to get us here without being arrested. If that had happened, we both would've been killed."

"Under whose orders?" Grouse asked.

Steve shrugged. "I'd bet, if you checked, you'd discover a lot of overtime put in by agents in Denver, Casper, Cheyenne and D.C., looking for a turncoat agent. Me. A couple of them flew on the same flight with us."

"I'll ask Miss—"

"Don't do that, sir. I think your secretary tried to get rid of us because someone asked her to make sure no one official got to you until they found me. She's probably being paid."

"I don't think so," Jessica said. "I think she's doing it for a deeper emotion than greed."

"What?" Steve asked.

"She's an old maid. I think someone has been flirting with her, probably Miguel Antonio. He sounds like the Latin lover type."

Steve looked skeptical.

Grouse's eyes widened again. "I have noticed him flirting with her. I meant to warn him not to do that, but he started talking about something else." He got up and paced back and forth several times. "Okay, how do I find out about the extra forces used the past couple of days if I don't use her?"

"Who else besides Miguel would know that you can trust?"

Grouse thought for a moment. "Jason Cadill. I trust him very much and he hates Miguel."

When he reached for the phone, however, Steve said, "Just a minute. Let me check your phone."

He unscrewed the speaker part of the phone and pulled out a small piece of equipment. "Here's part of the problem. Someone is recording your phone calls. Now go ahead."

Grouse stared at him. "I can't believe it! Who would've managed to plant that?"

"Either your secretary or Miguel himself." Steve gave him a steady look and Grouse nodded.

Both the men started checking the room, under lamps, under the tables and the edges of the desk. They found two more.

"I don't know what you want to do with these," Steve told him.

"Just stomp on them," Grouse advised.

"Does security ever sweep your office?" Steve asked.

"Miguel told me it would be a waste of time since no one but good guys ever got in here," Grouse said with a wry smile. "I guess he forgot about himself."

"I'd reinstate regular sweeps," Steve suggested.

After he'd stomped on the bugs, Steve put them in the trash in Grouse's private bath and closed the door. "Okay, make your call."

With a nod, he reached for his phone and dialed a number. "Jason? This is Walter. Did we have any agents on overtime here in D.C., Denver, Casper or Cheyenne the past couple of days?"

"I see." After a pause he said, "From my office? Yes, please, bring me a copy."

He hung up the phone. "He's coming up with a copy of a memo he received authorizing the manhunt for a drug dealer."

"You'd better let your secretary know," Jessica interjected. "You can tell her he's an old friend of Howie's father or you can say he's going to show us around. Either of those reasons will work without raising suspicions."

"You have a good imagination, young lady," Grouse said. Then he picked up his phone and called his secretary. He told her Jason had been friends with Howie's father and Howie wanted to meet him, too.

He hung up the phone and said, "I think she wasn't happy about that, but if he isn't shown in here in five minutes, I'm going out after him."

"Do you have any questions about what I've shown you?" Steve asked.

"No. It's very clear. What isn't so clear is linking Miguel to it."

"Have you seen his home?" Jessica asked.

"No, I haven't seen Jason's house, either, for that matter. What difference does that make?"

"That's one of the things Steve discovered easily. Can't you see what property is in Miguel's name?"

"Yes, I could. It may take a little time."

"May I use your computer?" Steve asked.

"Yes, of course." Grouse exchanged places with Steve.

"Steve, do you know his wife's name?" Jessica asked, her eyes narrowing as she stared at him.

"No. Do you, Mr. Grouse?"

"I believe it's Linda. I don't know her maiden name."

"I'll see what I can find," Steve said. He started the computer search, Grouse looking over his shoulder.

When they heard a knock on the door, Grouse opened it and invited a young man in. Then he shut the door firmly behind him.

"Jason Cadill, let me introduce Jessica Randall and Steve Carter."

The man's pleasant smile disappeared when he heard Steve's name.

"Sir! Steve Carter is who we were looking for the past few days!" He pulled his gun and pointed it at Steve.

"Put that gun away!" Grouse ordered.

"But—"

"Listen to me! Miguel told me over a week ago that Steve was dead. If he was lying to me, as is obvious by Steve's presence here, why?"

"He told us it was because Steve was a turncoat and he didn't want to admit that failure to you."

"Take my chair here and go through this information," Grouse told Steve and Jason.

Grouse stood by the window, watching the two men, while Jessica retired to the sofa against the wall.

"I'm glad you were able to stop him from shooting Steve," she told Grouse. "He deserves better than that." She smiled as Steve appeared to be totally involved in his search, not even fazed by Jason's earlier reaction.

"Yes, I would think so. He's been through a rough time, I would think, what with his injury and being pursued."

"Yes, but he never gave up. He said he had a job to do and he wouldn't quit until he could get to you and plead his case."

"I've found it!" Steve exclaimed.

"What did you find?" Grouse asked.

"Miguel and his wife have a 150-acre estate in Virginia."

"What is it worth?" Grouse asked, leaning forward.

"He bought it for twelve and a half million."

"What?" Jason gasped. "How did he afford that?"

Steve looked at him. "The same way my partners did. And I suspect Miguel has other operatives working for him in different areas."

"I told you Miguel was underhanded!" Jason exclaimed, looking at Grouse.

"I know you did, son, but you didn't bring me any evidence."

"I didn't think about looking for his house. Who would think he'd be that stupid?"

"People who manage to pull the wool over people's eyes get arrogant," Jessica said quietly. "Hollywood is full of them."

"So, now what, boss?" Jason asked, switching gears.

"Now we find out how many people Miguel has on his payroll. Starting with my secretary."

Jason frowned. "Is that why I couldn't get through to talk to you about the witch hunt?"

"When did you try?"

"When I first got the memo. What's the date on it?" he asked.

Grouse picked up the false memo. "It's dated almost a week ago. I think we need to call my secretary in here."

He rose and hit the button on the intercom. "Miss Carson, could you come in here, please?"

"Of course, sir."

She bustled in, full of self-importance. "Do you want me to escort this couple downstairs and get an agent to give them a tour?"

"No, Miss Carson, I don't think that will be necessary. Will you sit in this chair, please," Grouse said, patting the empty chair in front of his desk beside Jason. "Steve, if I may have my chair for a few minutes?"

"Of course, sir." Steve jumped up at once and moved to the sofa with Jessica.

Miss Carson watched their movement, confusion on her face.

Mr. Grouse settled in his chair and folded his hands on the desk before he looked at Miss Carson.

"Will you tell me who you work for?" he asked.

"Why, you, sir," she said with a smile.

"So I dictated this memo to you?" He slid the memo across the desk to her.

"Why, no, sir, Miguel…I mean Mr. Antonio gave it to me. He said it was what you wanted done."

"I see. Did he also tell you that I wanted to see no one on my staff for the past week?"

She didn't quite meet his gaze for her response. "Yes, sir."

"Is there anything else he told you?"

"N-no, sir." Her voice was now trembling.

"Did he ever come into my office when I wasn't here?"

"Well, he asked to use your office for a special call a couple of weeks ago. I didn't think you'd mind. He—he asked me not to mention that to you, but I think he was being silly."

"Did you stay in the office while he made the call?" Grouse asked gently.

"Why, no, sir! He wanted privacy."

"May I tell you what he was doing, Miss Carson?"

"Y-yes, sir."

"He was bugging my office and my telephone so that he had complete access to everything that went on here. And it's all thanks to you!"

"No! I wouldn't do that to you, Mr. Grouse! I promise!"

The three men stared at her, anger on their faces.

"I believe her," Jessica said softly.

"Come on, Jess, leave this to the professionals," Steve said, dismissing her comment.

"I suppose it was the professionals who got you here?" she snapped back.

"Look, Jess—"

"Why do you believe her?" Mr. Grouse asked.

"I believe she was foolish and unprofessional, but I don't believe she was trying to hurt you."

"She's right!" Miss Carson exclaimed. "I— He flattered me. I was lonesome and I thought—"

Beside her, Jason snapped, "You didn't think at all!"

"I think she could help us now," Jessica said.

"How?" Mr. Grouse asked.

"She could lure Miguel up here without rousing his suspicions."

Silence fell after Jessica's suggestion.

Finally, Mr. Grouse said, "Can you do that, Miss Carson?"

"Yes, sir! Of course, sir!"

"I'm not making any promises about your job, you understand. I have to be able to trust my secretary."

"Yes, sir," Miss Carson said with a sob.

"All right, call Miguel and get him up here."

"But—but I don't know what to say!" Miss Carson protested.

Everyone looked at Jessica.

"Why don't you tell him that Mr. Grouse has visitors that you think would be beneficial for him to meet if he just happened to drop by," Jessica suggested. "You might even whisper so he knows you're trying to conceal your activity."

"Yes, he'd expect that. I can do that."

Mr. Grouse waved her toward the phone. "Use this one."

With shaking fingers, she dialed Miguel Antonio's extension.

"Miguel? It's Abby. Mr. Grouse has the relatives of a high-powered senator in his office. I thought you might want to drop by and get introduced."

After a moment, she said, "I couldn't turn them away. They had an appointment."

They all watched as Miss Carson grew irritated. "Well, I'm sorry. I did my best. Just forget it." Then she hung up the phone. "That should get him here quickly," she said, with a grateful look at Jessica. "I really wasn't trying to hurt you, Mr. Grouse."

Grouse ignored her and looked at the two men. "We should've called for some guards first. I'll make that call," Mr. Grouse said, taking over the phone. He asked for four armed guards or four agents, whichever could be found first, to report to his office.

Just as he hung up, there was a knock on his door.

Everyone froze. Then as Mr. Grouse moved toward his office door, Steve and Jessica stood, as did Jason.

"Hi, Chief, I just thought I'd check in with you— Oh, I didn't know you had— Jason, what are you doing here?"

"Just checking in with the chief, like you," Jason said. "Come on in."

As Miguel came in, he saw Steve and Jessica standing to one side. "I don't believe I've met you two. I'm Miguel Antonio, one of the chief's underlings," he said with self-deprecating humor. "Are you visiting the capital?"

"Yes, we are," Steve said, "but not for the first time."

Something about Steve's voice stopped Miguel. "You know, you remind me quite a bit of a dear friend, one of our agents."

"Really?" Steve asked, playing along.

"Yes, he was unfortunately shot recently."

Jason took a step forward. "Was he? Are you talking about Steve Carter? I thought you told us he was a turncoat and had to be cut down if we found him."

Miguel glared at Jason before he sent an apologetic look at Grouse. "Sorry, boss, but I was hoping to keep my buddy's name clean...for his family, you know?"

"Yeah, 'cause I've got so much family, right, Miguel?" Steve drawled.

Miguel's head whipped around and he blinked several times as he stared at Steve. "If you had brown eyes, I'd think—"

Steve popped out his contact lens. "You mean, like this?"

Before anyone could move, Miguel pulled out his gun and grabbed Jessica, yanking her in front of his body. Then he put his gun to her head. "Take a step toward me and she dies."

Chapter Fifteen

Steve raised both hands. "Calm down, Miguel. You don't want to hurt her."

"No, amigo, I don't want to hurt the pretty lady, but I'm not going to die now, just when I've really hit the jackpot!" He sent an evil grin in Steve's direction.

"Miguel! Turn the woman loose. She's not going to be able to help you," Mr. Grouse ordered. But his order wasn't as effective as it had been with Jason.

"Sure she can, Walter," Miguel said. "She's going to be my shield. When I'm safely away, I'll probably let her go…unless she wants a little fun."

Jessica's eyes widened with fear. The man's hold was painful, but his words were even more so. She looked desperately at Steve.

Miguel gave a derisive laugh. "See, Steve? You shouldn't have come after me. I've got a lot more experience than you." He suddenly yanked Jessica backward toward the door.

Steve struggled to hold himself in place. He knew any movement might mean Jess's death.

It took only seconds for Miguel and Jessica to disappear, the door closing behind them.

As he headed for the door, Mr. Grouse ordered him to stop.

"But, sir, I've got to rescue Jessica!" Steve shouted.

"He'll still be out there, Steve. If you go out that door now, you'll be risking Jessica's life. I'm going to call the guards downstairs. They won't let him leave the building."

Steve returned, "Make that call. But I'm going after him!"

Jason followed Steve out the door.

Grouse was issuing an order as they left the room.

"Does Miguel park in the parking garage?" Steve asked Jason as they reached the elevator.

"Yeah, he does. Damn, I hope Walter thinks of that. There are no guards there."

The elevator opened up and they jumped in and pushed Basement, where the garage connected to the building.

"You should've at least gotten a gun, Steve," Jason pointed out.

"Never mind that. Call Grouse on your cell phone and alert him to where we're going."

Jason did. When Grouse's secretary answered, he passed on the message and hung up.

Just then, the elevator opened in the basement.

"What kind of car does he drive?"

"A black Mercedes. His space is just over—" He stopped when he saw the car moving, its tires squealing. "There he goes!" he hollered, pulling out his gun.

Steve shoved his arm down. "Don't shoot. You might accidentally hit Jessica. Is your car here?"

"Yeah, come on." He led the way to the next aisle. They both jumped in and followed Miguel's car.

JESSICA WAS NOW WEARING Miguel's handcuffs, her hands behind her back. He'd shoved her into the car, not worrying where she landed. She struggled to sit upright.

"Let me go now. You're free from them, so you don't need me anymore," she said, trying to keep her voice from trembling.

"Oh, no, little lady. We've got a ways to go before I let you go. When I do, you probably won't care anyway."

Jessica gulped, but she said nothing else. This man wouldn't be easy to persuade. Not with what he had to lose.

After a moment, though, she tried again. "You don't really have a choice, do you? I mean, how can you get your money out of your property? Unless you have an account out of the country."

"Of course I do, my dear. Do you think I'm stupid?" While he talked, he sped along, his gaze checking the rearview mirror frequently. "I have a lot put away. The guys in L.A. earned me a lot of money, but they weren't my only sources. I've been at this for a while."

"So let me go, and the search won't be so fierce!" she suggested.

"Don't think you're that important. They'll want to kill me. I pulled the wool over their eyes. They'll want revenge. And names. They'll definitely want names."

He pulled out a cell phone and hit a button on it before he held it to his ear. Speaking in Spanish, he gave rapid-fire orders into the phone.

Jessica wished she could speak Spanish, but she couldn't. The only word she thought she recognized was *helicopter*. But she could be mistaken.

He made a turn and seemed to suddenly be driving at a reasonable pace. She scooted closer to her door, sitting more upright. If he slowed for a stoplight, she might be able to get out of the car, if she could get the door open without drawing his attention to her—

"Get back over here!" he snapped.

Jessica froze. "I'm not going anywhere," she said. "I was just trying to sit up. This position is painful."

"I don't care about your pain. Stay next to me or I'll break some bones."

She was no coward, but she wasn't interested in being abused. She'd just have to hope Steve could come after her.

STEVE RAISED UP in his seat. "Is that them three cars ahead of us?"

"I think so, but I don't dare get any closer. He'd recognize my car and know we were after him."

Steve looked at Jason. "I think he'll know that, anyway."

"Maybe so, but I don't want to force him to do anything rash."

"Do you have any idea where he's going? This isn't toward Virginia."

"I guess he thought we'd figure where he was heading, so he's going in the opposite direction."

Steve thought about how Miguel would react. "No, I think he has an escape plan ready. He always planned ahead. He'd talk about always thinking ahead, figuring out what the bad guys would do. Remember?"

"Yeah, but…what would he do?"

"What airport are we heading to?"

"You think he'd go to one of the major airports? That wouldn't be too smart. We'd have a bulletin out for his arrest. He'd never make it onto a plane. Especially with Jessica with him."

"No. Small airports. Are there any small airports near here?"

"I don't know."

"Give me your cell phone."

Jason did as he said. Steve dialed Grouse's office number. "Mr. Grouse, this is Steve." He gave the man their location and asked if he could check on small airports in the area and see if Miguel had any airplanes of any kind reserved in his or Linda, his wife's, name.

Grouse called them back a couple of minutes later. There was a very small airport about fifteen minutes away from their location. Miguel, under his wife's name, had a helicopter hired there. They were taking off as soon as Miguel arrived.

"Have they filed a flight plan?"

"Yes, they're going to North Carolina."

"Thanks."

Steve directed Jason to try to catch up with Miguel's car. "We can't afford to let him get there ahead of us."

"But surely we could catch him before he got on the helicopter. He'll probably have Jessica with him."

"Oh, yeah, he'll have her with him. After he thinks he's gotten away, however, he'll toss her out midair. I'll never see her alive if he manages to get on the helicopter with her!"

Jason stared at him, his mouth agape, until Steve warned him to watch his driving. Steve's voice had reflected the pain in his heart at the thought of losing Jessica.

Jason immediately sped up, while Steve tried to contact the small airport. When the director answered, he told him not to allow the helicopter to leave, warning of a hostage situation and Miguel being wanted by the U.S. government.

"Take precautions. There'll be a woman with him, and he'll have a gun on her, I'm sure."

"I'll inform the pilot at once," the director agreed.

"Miguel is a trained pilot himself," Steve told him. "You'd better warn your pilot."

After he hung up the phone, Steve muttered, "Damn. I have a feeling he's planning on flying the copter himself, probably leaving the pilot knocked out on the ground."

He saw that they were directly behind the Mercedes. "Can you see any hint of Jessica?"

"Not so far. I thought I caught a glimpse of her blond hair, but she was yanked down at once if that was her."

Steve wanted to urge Jason to pass Miguel's car, but if the man didn't go to the airport, who knew where he was going. They couldn't afford to lose all trace of him.

The Mercedes turned onto a side road. Suddenly the car sped up, as if he had no fear of police patrolling the small road.

Jason had fallen back a bit, hoping Miguel wouldn't notice his car. In the meantime, he reached into his holster and pulled out his gun. "You'd better take this. I know you're going to be first out of the car. Miguel will try to take you out. At least the playing field will be level if you take my gun."

"Thanks," was Steve's only response other than to take the gun in his hand.

Instead of parking, the Mercedes plowed into the fence that surrounded the landing strip and headed for the helicopter waiting there.

"I guess he's not worried about his car," Jason muttered. "Hang on, I'm following him!"

They pulled alongside the Mercedes as it came to a halt in front of the helicopter. Steve leaped from Jason's car, the gun in one hand.

In the meantime, Miguel was pulling Jessica from the car. When he saw Steve pointing a gun at him, he pulled Jessica in front of him. "Don't shoot, Steve. Unless you want to kill her first just to get to me."

"Let her go, Miguel!"

"I can't do that, Steve. I've got plans."

"I'm sure you do."

"I'll let her go after we're away from here," Miguel said sweetly. "That's what you want, isn't it?"

"No. Because you're planning on throwing her out and letting her fall to her death!"

"Steve, how can you think such a thing of me? I'm surprised."

"Turn her loose now, Miguel!"

"Why? Because you have guards coming? Oh, no, you were in too much of a hurry, weren't you? Tsk, tsk, Steve, I've warned you about thinking ahead."

Steve moved forward as Miguel began dragging Jessica toward the chopper. "Jessica, don't get on the helicopter with him, whatever you have to do. He'll kill you if he gets you on board!"

"Now, don't scare the pretty lady, Steve." Miguel tightened his hold on Jessica's arm.

Suddenly, a woman appeared at the door of the helicopter. "Miguel!"

"It's all right. I'm coming. We'll be leaving now, Steve."

"I think not," a strange voice said, "unless you don't care about your wife." It was the pilot.

Miguel turned to look up. At the same time, Jessica threw herself down, and Steve charged Miguel.

But the pilot had overestimated Miguel's concern for his wife. Miguel fired immediately, hitting her point-blank in the chest. The bullet had to have traveled through her into the pilot, because he yelled out and fell back.

Steve immediately fired a shot into Miguel's chest that knocked him to the ground, causing him to drop his gun.

Jessica scrambled away from his body, her eyes wide with shock.

Even as he ran to Jessica's side, Steve shouted for Jason to call an ambulance.

"Are you okay, sweetheart?" he asked anxiously as he gathered her into his arms.

"Yes, but Miguel— Is he—"

"Yeah, unless my skills have eroded. Just a minute and I'll check." He felt for Miguel's pulse and found none. "He's dead, but I'd better check on that pilot."

He pulled Jess into a sitting position against the Mercedes. Then he moved to the door of the helicopter. He found Miguel's wife dead, but the man behind her had only a flesh wound. He was bleeding quite a bit, and Steve took off his shirt to bind the wound. Then he put his jacket back on.

Jason got out of the car after calling for backup and an ambulance. "What can I do?"

"Take the handcuffs off Jessica. Miguel and his wife are both dead."

While Jason did as he asked, Steve got the pilot out of the helicopter and headed toward the small building that housed the airport business office.

Once he had the man lying on the bunk bed in a back room, he hurried back out to find Jessica. She was sitting in Jason's back seat. Jason had the back door open and was talking to her. When Steve appeared at his side, he said, "She's not saying anything."

"Let me get in there with her. She's probably in shock."

Jason stepped away. "I'll go sit with the pilot and see if he can answer any questions until the ambulance gets here."

Steve scooted Jessica over and sat down beside her, putting his arm around her. "Are you all right?" he asked softly.

"Yes," she said faintly. "Jason was asking me questions and I just…couldn't answer him then. I'm okay now."

"I know you must've been scared. The man almost got away with everything."

"Yes. He—he was going to kill me. I had no idea how much I loved life until today." She nuzzled up against him until she realized he wasn't wearing a shirt. "Where's your shirt?"

"I took it off to bandage the pilot's wound. The bullet Miguel fired went through his wife and into the pilot."

"Oh, the poor woman!"

"Don't feel sorry for her. I don't think she believed Miguel was legitimately earning all that money they were spending."

"No. Probably not."

They both heard sirens pouring into the airport,

and Steve dropped a kiss on her forehead. "I've got to answer questions. I'll get back to you as soon as I can."

THAT WAS THE LAST she saw of Steve. Mr. Grouse was in one of the cars that arrived at the airport. When he realized she was sitting in the back of Jason's car, he came to her and asked where she wanted to go.

She knew Steve wouldn't be able to leave town until he'd helped settle the inquiry. And when he did get to leave, he'd be returning to Los Angeles.

She couldn't go there.

"I'd like to go home. To Wyoming."

"Very well. I can get you on the first plane to Denver. From there, you can get a flight to—"

"Casper. My family will pick me up there."

"Of course, I'll make sure that's arranged immediately. I want to thank you, my dear, for all your help. You saved a good man."

"And he saved me," she reminded Mr. Grouse.

Chapter Sixteen

When Mr. Grouse told Steve he'd sent Jessica home, Steve was as close to tears as he'd been in a long time. Somehow, he'd come to believe that his future, if he survived the trip to Washington, would be wonderful. He'd have a family, a wife, a real future. Not just days to survive.

"Thank you for getting her out of here, sir. She'll be safe back in Wyoming."

"My thoughts exactly. But she did say something about you saving her life."

"That was a debt I owed her many times over." Steve settled his teeth in his bottom lip and nodded to his chief. Then he turned away.

"Steve, I want you and Jason to go through Miguel's office and see what you can find. I suspect he had a Swiss bank account."

"He admitted as much, sir. I'll find Jason and get started on that job."

When he and Jason got back to the building, they went to Miguel's office. Dividing the room in two, they each began a thorough search of the room. They sent his secretary away after she admitted Miguel didn't confide in her and never let her file in his office without him there.

Steve was going through the bottom drawer of Miguel's desk, filled with spare office supplies. When he found nothing suspicious about the supplies, he shut the drawer. Then he realized the depth of the drawer didn't add up. He pulled it open again, unloaded the supplies and poked and prodded until he got the false bottom out of the drawer. Underneath, he found ledgers.

"Jason, come look at what I found." Inside the ledgers he found a list of agents with amounts and dates beside their names.

"I think you just found an important clue," Jason drawled. Then he frowned. "Damn, he had a lot of people working for him…and against us."

"Yeah. Like Marcus and Baldwin."

"What's in the other ledger?"

Steve opened the book. "It looks like it contains daily balances." He whistled as he read the totals. "Look at the amounts we're talking about, Jason. Even a saint would be tempted."

"We've got to talk to Grouse at once. Are there any account numbers?"

Steve flipped back to the front of the ledger. "Here they are. Maybe the government can claim the money."

"Let's go show Walter."

SEVERAL DAYS LATER, things were wrapping up. It was obvious that Baldwin had cut and run. They'd found his and his wife's names on a flight out to South America.

Other men who hadn't heard of Miguel's death were easily arrested. Grouse thought they were going to be able to claim the huge amount of money in Miguel's accounts.

There were a lot of spots to fill, which meant a hiring splurge, which would benefit those on the waiting list. But before they began hiring, Walter Grouse called all his agents to a meeting. There, for those who still didn't know, he explained about the recent events. He thanked them for their honorable behavior. Then he told them he had many openings. He wanted to be sure that the new people would be working with an experienced man, so he offered them the opportunity to apply for other locations.

Steve sat there, thinking about what he should do. If he were honest, he wanted to quit. After all, none of the openings were in Wyoming.

But that would be abandoning the ship.

He sighed. Then, as Grouse seemed to be ending the meeting, he decided he should say something.

Before he could, Walter turned to him. "Steve, there are a couple of men wanting to talk to you in my office."

Puzzled, Steve asked who they were.

"I think you'll understand when you get to my office."

Steve didn't ask any more questions. He stood and left the meeting room.

THREE DAYS LATER, Jessica was talking to the Rawhide eighth grade class. She'd already talked to the current high school students. She was explaining the opportunity to join the drama class and drama club. She'd intended to be enthusiastic with them, but she hadn't realized it would be so difficult to show that upbeat emotion.

She'd been caught in a dismal argument between her head and her heart. She wanted a life with Steve, but she didn't want a life in Los Angeles. And she couldn't have one without the other.

With a silent sigh, she straightened her shoulders and faced the young group. "For those of you who don't know me, I grew up here in Rawhide. And I think you're lucky to be here, too. But I was always a little different from my family and friends. I wanted to try acting. We didn't have any opportunities here in town, so I went to Hollywood."

That got their attention.

"I lived there for three years, supported by my parents who actually believed in me. In those three years, I learned the acting trade well enough to get a few roles on television. Then I landed an ingenue role in a big movie."

The young audience drew their breaths.

"As soon as I finished that movie, I knew I could come back to Rawhide, because I'd proved myself. But I hope to offer the students in Rawhide an opportunity right here. So I'm starting drama classes and a club that will put on performances for our community."

"Will you be the teacher?" one young girl called out, catching Jessica by surprise.

She swallowed before she answered. "Yes, at least for the first year," she said as the back door to the room opened. To her surprise, a lot of her family came into the room.

She smiled at them. "Boys and girls, looks like my family came here to support me." She found herself trembling, near tears, at the support her family was giving her once again.

She had almost turned back to her listeners when the door at the back of the room opened one more time.

Frozen in place, all she could do was stare at the man who stood there. The man she thought she'd lost.

"S-Steve?" she whispered. All the kids turned

around again to stare at him. That convinced Jessica that she wasn't looking at a mirage, a dream. She'd seen him in her sleep a jillion times.

Now he was here in person.

He moved toward the front of the room...and her.

All she could do was stare at him. She was afraid if he got too close, she'd throw herself at him.

Then her gaze met her father's.

Her father was smiling at her. He'd been out of town on business a few days now. In fact, when she'd left for the school, he still hadn't come back. How strange that he would turn up the same time as Steve.

Steve stepped to Jessica's side and took her hand. "Does anyone have any questions for Miss Randall? I can promise she's a really good actress."

There were one or two questions before the teachers told the students they had to go back to class.

Jessica watched them file out. They'd only gotten part of the way out of the room when Steve pulled her into his arms and kissed her.

She pushed herself out of his hold, knowing if she didn't, she'd never be able to leave him again.

"Steve, what are you doing here?"

"Reporting for duty, sweetheart," he whispered.

"What are you talking about?"

"I'm going to be working in Wyoming now. And I hoped you might be interested in a future with me."

"You mean—"

"Will you marry me?"

"Oh, yes! Yes, I'll marry you! I've been hurting so much since I came back from D.C."

She fell into his arms, sobbing against his chest.

"Hush, honey, or your family won't believe you're happy."

Jessica lifted her head off his chest and turned to stare at the back of the room. "Why are they here?" she asked with a sniff.

Her father stepped closer to them. "We're here to celebrate your engagement, honey. We approve."

"But how did you know? Steve just—"

"Your dad and Mike came to D.C. to ask for help in Wyoming. They said I was desperately needed here to raise morale." Steve shook Brett's hand.

With a beaming smile, Jessica looked at Steve. "If it's my morale you're talking about, they're absolutely right."

"Walter Grouse agreed with them. So here I am, if you'll take me."

"Didn't I already say yes?" she asked, wrapping her arms around his neck.

"Yeah, but I think we'd better delay the celebration until we're alone," Steve suggested.

"Not a chance. If my family went to so much trouble to trap you for me, there's no way I'm going to let you go."

"Oh, well, I guess they won't mind if I kiss you properly, then," Steve said, "because I'm not letting you go, either."

Epilogue

Jessica was giving a great performance. She was sitting on a stool in the audience, watching a high school play practice that desperately needed work. But she didn't want to hurt the actors' feelings.

Just as they finished the scene, her water broke. Though it had taken her by surprise, she'd prepared. She motioned for one of her senior students, Jennifer, who came running over.

"Jen, go call the hospital and tell Jon I said it's time for him please to come get me and call Steve." Before Jennifer could run away, she pulled her to a stop. "First, dismiss the group and ask them to return to their classrooms."

Jennifer made quick work of her orders and returned to Jessica's side and helped her down from the stool. "The doctor said he'd be right here. Shall we go out and meet him?"

"Yes, of course," Jessica agreed through gritted teeth as a pain gripped her belly.

Before they could reach the door, it swung open and Steve hurried to her side.

"What are you doing here? I thought you were out of town." Jessica leaned against him.

"I finished early. Jon called the sheriff's office to find out where I was. Luckily I was visiting with Mike. Come on, Jon's almost here."

He swung her into his arms, thanked Jennifer for her help and carried his wife out to Jon's car.

A few hours later, Steve was staring in awe at his son, wrapped in Jessica's arms.

Steve put his arm around both of them. "Sweetheart, you were so brave, and you gave birth to the best-looking baby in the world."

"Be careful. Remember most of the family has already had babies they considered beautiful," she teased.

"Okay, we'll keep it a secret that they're wrong," he assured her with a grin. Then, in a more serious light, he said, "You've given me the most wonderful future in the world. I love you so much."

If you enjoyed what you just read,
then we've got an offer you can't resist!

Take 2 bestselling
love stories FREE!
Plus get a FREE surprise gift!

Clip this page and mail it to Harlequin Reader Service®

IN U.S.A.	IN CANADA
3010 Walden Ave.	P.O. Box 609
P.O. Box 1867	Fort Erie, Ontario
Buffalo, N.Y. 14240-1867	L2A 5X3

YES! Please send me 2 free Harlequin Intrigue® novels and my free surprise gift. After receiving them, if I don't wish to receive anymore, I can return the shipping statement marked cancel. If I don't cancel, I will receive 4 brand-new novels each month, before they're available in stores! In the U.S.A., bill me at the bargain price of $4.24 plus 25¢ shipping and handling per book and applicable sales tax, if any*. In Canada, bill me at the bargain price of $4.99 plus 25¢ shipping and handling per book and applicable taxes**. That's the complete price and a savings of at least 10% off the cover prices—what a great deal! I understand that accepting the 2 free books and gift places me under no obligation ever to buy any books. I can always return a shipment and cancel at any time. Even if I never buy another book from Harlequin, the 2 free books and gift are mine to keep forever.

181 HDN DZ7N
381 HDN DZ7P

Name	(PLEASE PRINT)	
Address	Apt.#	
City	State/Prov.	Zip/Postal Code

Not valid to current Harlequin Intrigue® subscribers.

Want to try two free books from another series?
Call 1-800-873-8635 or visit www.morefreebooks.com.

* Terms and prices subject to change without notice. Sales tax applicable in N.Y.
** Canadian residents will be charged applicable provincial taxes and GST.
All orders subject to approval. Offer limited to one per household.
® are registered trademarks owned and used by the trademark owner and or its licensee.

INT04R   ©2004 Harlequin Enterprises Limited

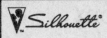

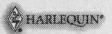
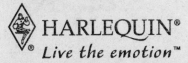